COWBOY PRIDE

LACY WILLIAMS

1

"Everyone knows a rancher in possession of a large spread needs a wife."

At Mama's outlandish statement, Liza Bennett glanced up from the measurement she was taking of a stirrup strap. Her sister Janie, who was sorting belt buckles into two small bins, didn't look up. They worked together in the storeroom of Bennett's Leather Goods, Cobbler and Saddlery. Calvin, Wyoming's, finest, and only, store of its kind.

From the table where she worked, Liza could see to the front where Mama was leaning over the display counter, speaking loudly enough that her voice carried throughout the store. And, Liza was sure, to the horses hitched out front.

Lydia and Kitty, Liza and Janie's younger sisters, were supposed to be tagging an assortment of items to be put on display, but their task remained forgotten in the excitement of Mama's topic of conversation.

Fortunately for Liza's—and her sisters'—reputations, the shop was nearly empty. Martha Stoll, Mama's closest friend and the biggest gossip in town, was the only shopper at the moment.

Unfortunately for the family's income, the shop was empty except for the gossipy woman.

Liza frowned, determined to concentrate on her project. She had the sense that her older sister was listening just as raptly as the younger ones were, though Janie's head remained down.

Or not.

After Albert Rogers had jilted Janie and his mother had run them out of Cottonwood Cove, Janie's naturally bashful nature had worsened into intense shyness. Often Liza couldn't tell what her quiet sister was thinking.

Mama was determined to make an advantageous match for each of her daughters.

Liza was just as determined to ensure Mama couldn't humiliate Janie with her sometimes outrageous antics. Meanwhile, Liza would find her sister the perfect man.

It was the least she could do, after all.

"...he's all set to arrive on the afternoon train," Mama was saying now. "Hopefully he'll come to the dance hall tonight, and the girls can meet him then."

"Who's coming, Mama?" Lydia bounced, unable to contain her excitement.

"The man buying the Parrott spread, dear."

Two years ago, a prominent local rancher, Joe Parrott, had been implicated in the murder of the local marshal and attempted murder of the man's wife, the new marshal, Danna O'Grady. Parrott's property had remained unsold—until now?

Mama leaned further over the counter, maybe trying to lower her voice, though it still carried throughout the shop. "His name is Nathan Bingley, and if he can afford the Parrott spread, he must be well off. The perfect catch for one of you girls."

The bell above the shop door jangled, and Liza looked up

sharply, expecting to shush her mother as a customer entered. Instead, Liza caught sight of a set of broad shoulders and a head of dark hair as a man strode away.

Had someone been loitering in the corner of the shop? Had Mama been gossiping in the presence of a real customer?

Liza ground her teeth. The shop was failing, and Mama didn't seem to care. Despite the door having just opened, Mama's mouth hadn't slowed. She was now extolling the virtues of the large ranch.

Liza forced herself to focus on each pencil stroke as she crafted a matching pattern for the stirrup that was nearly worn through. There wasn't anything she could do about the offended customer now. But she would speak to Papa later about Mama's actions. If she wouldn't curb her tongue, she should stay out of the shop.

Mama had no idea that her run-on mouth was only making life harder for the sisters. Liza's determination to help Janie find a match would be tested at the town dance later tonight.

"I think your blue poplin will be perfect for tonight," Liza said offhandedly to Janie. "It highlights the blue of your eyes."

Janie didn't look up as she tossed two brass buckles into a bin. "I was thinking of staying home."

"You must go." Liza didn't know or care about this Nathan character, but she knew that two eligible young men—the banker's son and a young widower who owned a homestead south of town—would be in attendance, and she was determined Janie should be introduced to them.

But she couldn't tell Janie that.

"If you don't come, Mama will turn all her matchmaking attentions on me."

Janie looked up at this, a tiny smile playing on her lips. "A definite benefit of staying home."

"Janie, please come. At least if we band together, we can help each other avoid Mama's machinations."

Janie was considering it. Liza could tell by the slight tilt of her head.

"You're my dearest sister." Liza pressed her advantage. "Don't abandon me to Mama tonight." Liza knew it was cheating to play on her sister's sympathies, but if she left Janie to her own devices, she would be a spinster in no time.

"Fine," Janie said. "For an hour, only."

"An hour."

It would have to be enough.

"AND WE BECOME prey for the buzzards," Rob Darcy murmured as he entered the town dance hall. He'd been told the multi-purpose building was used for many events, including Sunday morning worship services, fundraisers and the like.

But tonight's event was the worst. A town dance. It had been planned to allow the entire population to mingle.

"What was that?" his friend Nathan asked.

"Nothing." Rob knew better than to use sarcasm with his friend. Nathan was too much of a straight-shooter to catch it.

Rob felt the weight of dozens of stares as the corner of the dance hall where they'd walked in quieted. No surprise. He and Nathan were strangers. Conspicuous.

Of course the dance had been scheduled for the day of their arrival, when Rob was worn slick from the train journey, having been crowded into a passenger car like so many cattle. He wanted nothing more than to sit in a rocker near a fireplace with a cup of coffee. And retire early.

Nathan—who was more a brother than a friend—had been invited to the dance no fewer than five times. And since Nathan was jovial and kind, of course he'd wanted to come.

And then there was Mindy, Nathan's half-sister. Though they hadn't known each other long, Nathan would do anything to make the seventeen-year old happy. Including escorting her to tonight's dance in an attempt to win a smile.

Rob tapped his hat against his thigh. If he were lucky, he'd make an escape before too long. He didn't want to relinquish his favorite dress Stetson. Perhaps he could hide out at his sister and brother-in-law's home until he could return to the ranch Nathan was considering for purchase.

Nate was already drawing curious and flirtatious glances from several women as he circled among the crowd. Rob wanted to groan.

Perhaps he wouldn't have an early escape. Nate was handsome and drew women like flies to honey. But after Rob had helped Nate discover his fiancé's duplicitous behavior, Rob had come to realize that Nate needed help determining women's true motivations.

Which was humorous only because of Rob's history.

Nevertheless, he was determined not to let Nate get hurt again.

And if that meant fending off the local women until Nate settled in Calvin, Rob would do his duty. He owed his friend nothing less.

"How long do we have to stay in this hick town?" Mindy's nose twitched as if she'd smelled something rotten. "The prospects here are disappointing."

Rob ignored her even as Nate attempted to soothe her.

It didn't work. She turned away from her brother, crossing her arms over her middle.

The crush of bodies inside the large hall was stifling, made worse by the scents of too much pomade and rose water.

They were quickly besieged by folks wanting introductions. So many that Rob couldn't remember half the names.

Nate didn't seem to have that problem, jovial and unruffled as always. So Rob noticed immediately when Nathan froze.

"What's the matter?" Rob glanced around for the person who could've elicited such a strong reaction from his unflappable friend.

"There, by the punchbowl," Nate murmured. "No, don't stare! She'll see you."

"You must be joking," Mindy said.

Rob did his best to glance sparingly in the direction Nate indicated.

He, too, froze when he found himself caught in a pair of fathomless brown eyes. Attraction sparked in a way he'd never felt before.

He fought the urge to go to the woman, to wrangle an introduction, and then to find a quiet corner where they could get to know each other.

But his loyalty to Nate went deeper than a pretty face. He forced himself to turn to his friend and ask, "The brunette?"

"The blonde," came Nate's swift response. "She's captivating."

Rob looked again, probably less surreptitiously than Nate had hoped, and searched for a blonde woman. *Not* the brunette.

He refused to acknowledge the cinch that eased from around his chest, allowing him to breathe again.

Again, he met a pair of intelligent dark eyes. There did seem to be a blonde the periphery of his vision, but he couldn't tear his gaze away—

Was she laughing? There seemed to be a definite spark of humor in the depths of her eyes.

"Let's go over," he heard himself say.

He was unaccustomed to the sensations traveling up his spine as he navigated the crowd, Nate by his side.

Strangely, the dread he usually felt in the presence of a pretty girl was absent. All he felt was anticipation.

And then he caught sight of the matronly woman standing between the girls.

The same woman whose shrill, social-climbing mouth had caused him to abandon the leather goods store.

2

"He's coming over here!" Janie murmured beneath her breath.

"Ow!" Liza rubbed the inside of her upper arm, where her sister had just pinched her. Mama was wearing too much cologne, and she wished for a breath of fresh outside air.

"Wait, they're stopping."

Liza's heart banged against her ribcage. "Who?" She looked at the crowd and tried to figure out who Janie was looking at.

Surely not the dark-haired man. The handsome one with the shadow of stubble at his jaw and the intense eyes.

"That's Mr. Bingley," Mama gasped. "The blond man. And his sister with him."

Liza glanced at Janie beside her. Her fair-skinned sister was blushing. Janie was interested in someone. Perfect.

Another glance into the crowd showed that the dark man was in fact accompanying the fair-haired siblings. Curiosity peaked. Who was he?

Mama was speaking again. "The man with them is Rob Darcy. He's rumored to be even richer than Mr. Bingley, supposed to have a nice ranch up near Sheridan."

Mama was getting excited, and Liza felt herself coloring as Mama's voice rose.

And kept rising. "And he's the marshal's brother."

It seemed Liza's fear that her mother would be overheard was well-founded, because Mr. Darcy grimaced as the trio neared.

As usual, Mama was oblivious. She reached out for the men before they'd finished their approach. Liza turned her head at the last moment. She couldn't watch.

"Mr. Bingley. Mr. Darcy. What an honor to meet you," Mama bubbled. "I am Maude Bennett. My husband owns the leather goods shop here in Calvin. These are my two oldest daughters, Janie and Liza."

Liza faced the men, feeling as if she were moving through a vat of molasses. Goose-pimples crawled up her arms. She lifted her eyes.

Her gaze collided with Rob Darcy's. Time stilled. His eyes spoke to her.

Vaguely, as if from a far distance, she heard Mr. Bingley say, "My sister, Mindy."

Liza still couldn't look away from Mr. Darcy. Something passed between them, a moment of connection, as if he were a kindred spirit.

And then her mother's voice broke into the moment.

"My two youngest daughters are already dancing."

Shaken, trembling but attempting to cover it, Liza glanced at Janie, who stared at Nathan Bingley with rapt attention. While Mr. Bingley was certainly attractive, Mr. Darcy was something more. Rugged, handsome. Intense. He was a bit older than she'd first thought; tiny lines fanned from the corners of his eyes as if he spent time outdoors.

"Would you share a dance with me?" Mr. Bingley swept

Janie into the swirling crowd, leaving his sister behind and Mr. Darcy at Liza's side.

She waited for a similar invitation, but none was forthcoming. Finally, Liza asked, "Do you enjoy dancing, Mr. Darcy?"

"Not as a rule."

Stung at his cool tone, Liza turned back to look at the dancers, but not before she saw Mindy Bingley's faint smirk.

Maybe he hadn't felt anything at all. Maybe Liza's imagination had run away with her. Before she'd known how dire the situation was for Papa's store, she'd loved to spend afternoons reading, lost in fanciful imaginations. Perhaps the connection she thought she'd felt had only been in her head.

Liza made herself keep her gaze forward. She found Janie in the crowd. Her sister beamed up at Nathan Bingley. Janie was practically glowing.

And Mr. Bingley seemed to return the sentiment. He stared down at Janie as if she were a treasure he'd found after searching his entire life.

Perhaps here was a man worthy of her sister. It was too soon to tell, but Liza would hope so, for her sister's sake.

Nearby, Mama's voice rattled over the sounds of the crowd, slightly discordant. Distracted by neighbors and friends, she was soon safely away from Mr. Darcy and Miss Bingley.

Liza loved her mother dearly, but she refused to allow Janie to be embarrassed. Not tonight. Liza could corral Mama and keep her away from Nathan Bingley, at least until he had adequate time to become smitten with Janie. Judging by his expression, it shouldn't take long.

She left the still-silent Mr. Darcy and his companion behind, a little knot in her stomach urging her to remain, imagined connection or not.

But Janie's happiness was more important than Liza's imaginations.

. . .

NATHAN'S HEART raced as Janie twirled in his arms and the music from the fiddle and banjo faded away.

She beamed up at him, her cheeks flushed and one blond curl escaping from her coif to lie against her cheek.

His heart galloped like a horse that'd tossed its rider and run free. Meeting someone was not in his plan. What was he doing?

Some of the quick trepidation must've shown, because her expression clouded over, the beautiful smile muted.

"Thank you for the dance," she said so softly that he was more reading the words on her lips than hearing them over the cacophony of voices in the crowded room.

He didn't want her to walk away. He wanted to see her smile return.

"Does your father own land nearby?" he asked. If she lived close enough to the Parrott ranch, he might come calling.

"Papa owns the saddlery in town. We sell leather goods of all sorts. And do repairs."

That's right. A shopkeeper's daughter. Her mother had mentioned that in her brief introduction.

"Ah. You probably meet a lot of folks, then." What he really wanted to ask was whether she had a beau. Whether one of the many cowboys or rancher's sons or bankers stopped in at the store regularly to chat and flirt.

But he wasn't quite sure how to word it without being presumptuous.

"And you've come to consider purchasing the Parrott land?"

For a moment, unease flared at her innocent question. Remembering Hildy as she clung to his arm at a dance just like this... He blinked the memory away.

Janie Bennett was not like Hildy. Probably not.

He didn't actually know Janie. She seemed innocent enough. Perhaps she'd voiced the question to be polite.

The fortune-hunters were the reason he and Rob had circulated the rumor that he was only viewing the Parrott spread. In fact, he'd already purchased the land, a few stock horses, and all the cattle outright.

It had been Rob's idea. And Nathan valued his friend's advice more than anything else. Rob was five years older, and Nathan had worked on his spread in northern Wyoming for years. While the other cowhands had come and gone, some settling on their own homesteads, some drifting off to find more adventure, Nathan had stayed.

He'd had nowhere else to go.

When his half-sister Mindy had arrived on Rob's doorstep months ago with a letter and news of Nathan's inheritance, it had been a shock. Rob had advised him and come up with the plan to put Nathan's funds to work. He'd believed in Nathan when no one else ever had.

"Miss Bennett, can I have a dance?" A cowboy in a simple blue shirt and denims stood beside them.

Nathan realized he'd wandered off in his own thoughts and that her smile had faltered further.

And then an older woman, a mama with a gleam in her eye who made him want to recoil, approached from Nathan's other side.

"Mr. Bingley. Oh, Mr. Bingley, allow me to introduce my daughter..."

Politeness dictated that he smile at her. Over her shoulder, he saw Janie glance back at him, and he nodded to her.

He wanted to dance with her again.

Wanted to have a longer conversation.

Wanted her all to himself.

. . .

"WHAT A DREADFUL EVENT," Mindy said. "I've had enough of rough cowhands."

Rob agreed. After two hours of making small talk, his patience was used up. Give him a lariat, branding iron, or shovel. He excelled at ranching. He'd never gained mastery over social graces. He blamed his upbringing—too many years spent isolated on a ranch when he was young.

Miss Liza Bennett had kept a good distance between them since that horrid introduction.

He'd felt a keen, queer sense of loss when she'd slipped through the crowd, drawing her mother away by the arm. As if she'd escaped with most of the room's light in her smile. It was dim without her near.

Until now, he'd been acutely aware of her presence in the room. She danced almost as often as she laughed. She had a distinct, tinkling way of expressing her merriment. She swirled through the large room, effervescent with joy.

It made him feel old.

He was likely a decade her senior, but the difference seemed starker in light of her joy.

Once, he'd almost gathered his courage to ask her to dance.

Which was patently ridiculous. If her gold-digging mother got any hint of his attraction to her daughter, he'd be like a horse pursued like a persistent horse-fly. Bad enough that Nathan had danced with her sister. Multiple times.

Nathan didn't seem to think the night had been wasted. He couldn't seem to tear his eyes away from Janie Bennett. Janie was indeed nice to look at, but she was nothing compared to her sister.

Not that Rob would do anything about it. He might have a large, beautiful spread, but he had nothing to offer a woman like Liza Bennett.

Better to focus on Nate, the reason he'd come.

Mindy snagged her brother by the arm and dragged him through the door. Nate seemed surprised to find the crowd dispersing out of the dance hall and into the street, where they were waving goodbyes and heading back to their homes.

"What fun!" Nate crowed. "I think I danced every dance." Most with Janie Bennett. Rob had yet to determine if that was a good or bad thing.

"You did." But Rob couldn't begrudge his friend a good time, even if he'd been miserable. That's what he got for thinking so much.

Nate grinned. "No wonder I've got a blister inside my boot." He slapped Rob's shoulder. "You should've danced more—"

"Or at all," Mindy mumbled.

Rob ignored her. She was Nate's problem, not his.

"There were an awful lot of pretty girls," Nate continued, seeming not to hear his sister. "Like Janie's sister." Nate smiled slyly.

For a moment, Rob wondered if Nate had seen the instant connection between himself and Liza Bennett. Which made him wonder if *she'd* noticed. Surely not.

But a glance at Nate showed he was lost in thought. Probably thinking of Janie. Redirection was definitely called for.

"She was passable. Maybe if she'd been more of a temptation, I would've danced with her."

Mindy's eyes cut behind his shoulder, and Rob turned his head—just in time to lock gazes with the very girl he'd just spoken of. The Bennett family must've exited the dance hall just after the Bingleys had.

He winced as the tic in her jaw made it clear she'd heard every word, though none of her sisters or mother seemed to be paying attention.

Even he knew that insulting the fairer sex was uncouth.

He braced himself for a tearful scene, but she only turned her face away and walked down the boardwalk with her family.

He stared after her as Nate handed Mindy into the buggy.

This was further evidence of what he already knew. He wasn't gentle enough, had no social graces to woo a woman. He'd given up on making a match long ago. Right after he'd nearly killed his younger sister.

He didn't understand women. Never would.

Better to keep a safe distance.

3

"...And then he said I was passable." Liza laughed, though she hadn't found the insult amusing last night. Someone so conceited deserved to be laughed at.

Obviously, the attraction she'd felt for Rob Darcy had been one-sided. She'd told Janie all of it last night in the privacy of their tiny bedroom above the shop, whispering so Lydia and Kitty wouldn't hear from their bed wedged just across.

Now, morning sunlight streamed through the front windows of Papa's store. Liza bent over Papa's accounts ledger, wishing Mama would take the younger girls upstairs and leave her in peace. Attempting to decipher Papa's scribbled handwriting made her head hurt enough.

And she wanted to get Janie alone to talk about Nathan Bingley.

"It's too bad," Kitty lamented. "We heard the Darcy ranch is as big as half of Converse County." She fiddled with the sleeve of her dress, ignoring the boots behind the counter that needed to be re-shelved.

"Land and cattle aren't everything," Liza chided. "Imagine waking up to a bear like him every morning."

Her sisters pealed with laughter, and their merriment was worth the slight humiliation she'd suffered last night.

In the grand scheme of things, it didn't matter. It wasn't as if she was likely to see him again. Maybe in passing, or as a customer in the shop. She was determined to forget about it, forget about him.

Concentrate on Janie, who'd come out of her bashful shell last night. Now Janie leaned her chin on one hand, absent-mindedly ticking a pencil against the countertop, lost in her own thoughts.

"Mr. Bingley is so handsome," Lydia said slyly. "Don't you think, Janie?"

Janie straightened, cutting her eyes low.

"He danced with Janie more than anyone else," Mama reminded no one in particular. It was the fifth time she'd said as much this morning.

Before Liza could divert the conversation, a small boy banged into the store.

"Gotsa note for ya here, Miss Janie," he said, waving a folded paper above his head.

"Who is it from?" Kitty demanded.

"I want to see it," Lydia called out, dancing out from behind the counter.

"Girls," Mama admonished as she reached for the boy who now appeared overwhelmed and frozen where he stood.

Before any of the three of them could as much as get a finger on the missive, Janie had whirled between a saddle display and a shelf full of boots and snatched it from the boy's fingers. She pressed a penny into his hand. "Thank you."

"Who sent the note?" Mama asked the boy.

He shrugged, looking over his shoulder like he wanted badly to escape. "Someone out at the Parrott place. My pa was there earlier delivering some feed, and the note got sent back with him."

Mama gasped, giving him an opening. He ran for the door.

Janie unfolded the note, quickly scanning its contents.

"From Mr. Bingley?" Mama demanded before Janie could possibly have had time to read it.

The two younger girls looked on, wide-eyed. While Mama's speculation and outlandish expectations were one thing, this was real.

Liza's stomach tightened with nerves on her sister's behalf.

"It's from Mindy," Janie finally murmured to the expectant room, eyes still on the paper. "She wants me to come for tea this afternoon."

"Tea?" Liza mouthed.

Mama hooted and Kitty and Lydia giggled.

"Her brother won't be present."

The room went silent at Janie's pronouncement.

"What do you mean?" Mama trilled, voice going high—a sure sign of distress.

"It only says he'll be busy with the ranch," Janie murmured. She tucked the note into the pocket of her dress.

"I didn't know you'd spoken to Miss Bingley last night," Liza put in, hoping to distract Janie from their mother's irrational frustration.

"Yes, a bit in between dances. She seemed friendly enough."

Liza couldn't agree. She'd thought Miss Bingley standoffish, and not just because she'd laughed at Rob Darcy's *passable* comment. But Janie always wanted to think the best of people, so Liza held her tongue.

"Mama, may I take the buggy?"

Their mother looked up from where she'd been staring out the front window, as if Janie's question surprised her.

"No. No, I don't think so. You can go on horseback."

"What? Mama, no." Liza touched Mama's arm. Janie could handle a buggy, but she wasn't terribly comfortable in the saddle.

"If Janie wants to go badly enough, she may go on horseback. Lydia, why don't you run down to the livery and have Will saddle up our mare?"

Janie had gone pale, but her mouth had firmed with determination. Liza knew that look. Her sister would go to the Parrott spread for dinner with Miss Bingley regardless of her own discomfort. But what was the point of Mama's insistence that she ride and not take the buggy?

"Liza, come help me dress," Janie said, grasping her arm with a tug toward the stairs behind the store.

Liza allowed one more look to her mother, hoping to convey her disapproval. Behind Mama, out the window, the sky above the Laramie Mountains had grown gray.

BUCKLES SHIFTED NERVOUSLY, and Janie clutched the saddle knob with both hands, the reins slipping in her gloved fingers. The ground was so very far away.

She must keep control.

She'd borrowed one of Liza's split riding skirts. The material felt heavy against her legs, pressing her limbs into the animal.

She hated riding.

Perhaps she should have insisted she be allowed to take the two-seated buggy. Or perhaps she should have used some of her meager allowance to rent a wagon from the livery.

Anything but this.

She should learn to be more assertive. Were there lessons for that sort of thing?

Clouds hung low on the horizon, and the air was oppressive and moist. Where was the crossing? She remembered the bridge. She'd been nervous the last time Papa had driven the family wagon across the rickety structure. This weather wasn't helping her nerves. The sooner she reached the Parrott's old ranch, the better.

Even if Nathan Bingley wouldn't be there.

She hadn't expected the way he'd made her feel last night. For two years, she'd kept a careful distance from men who wanted to come calling.

Until Nathan.

He'd swept away her fears, her innate shyness, without even trying. Made something indefinable roll through her entire body, like the rumbling thunder that was rolling through the sky now—

She'd lived on the Wyoming plain long enough to fear flash floods and rogue lightning strikes. She needed to reach the Parrott place, and thinking about Nathan Bingley was only a distraction.

Where was that bridge? There—

She urged Buckles forward, and the horse carefully picked the first steps over the rickety wooden structure. She didn't like the look of the water beneath them, boiling up, the color of brown clay. A tree limb floated past, and she swallowed hard.

"It's—it's all right," she said softly to the horse.

The town council had spoken of rebuilding the bridge, but most of the time the creek was placid and low and it was easy enough to cross on horseback or even on foot.

Not so today.

She held her breath as the horse's weight caused the bridge to shift and creak.

Perhaps this errand was foolishness after all. With Mama's

maneuvers, it could appear Janie was chasing the handsome rancher-to-be.

And after the accusations Albert and his mother had leveled at her, she couldn't afford—

Her roiling thoughts were broken as one of the support beams gave way and the bridge wobbled like it was made of children's blocks.

For one prolonged moment, she was suspended in mid-air, atop the horse, her heart beating frantically as she sought a way to escape the inevitable.

And then the bridge crumbled.

She lurched to the side, trying to extricate herself from the horse.

She tumbled into the water without even time to take a breath.

Water closed over her head, so icy that it stole her breath.

The heavy split skirts tangled around her legs, their sodden weight making it impossible to kick. Her boots were filled with water.

Darkness surrounded her, the swirling current forcing her to contort in directions she couldn't fathom.

Her head broke the surface, and she gasped a desperate breath through her hair, which had fallen out of its pins and clung to her head like slimy, muddy tentacles.

Where was the horse? It might be her only chance to escape the floodwaters.

She pried her eyes open only to see a tangled mass of roots ahead, so close that she was flung against them.

She reached out, trying to grasp hold of anything that might save her.

The current pulled and yanked like a monster bent on its prize, but she caught hold of a branch.

Her arm wrenched, and she cried out as pain blinded her, sent stars over her vision.

She lost her grip on the branch. The weight of her skirts pulled her under.

Everything went black.

4

Nathan considered himself an intelligent man, though most of his smarts had been obtained in the school of hard knocks.

He got through life well enough, especially since the day Rob had given him a job on his ranch.

But he was stymied with how to reach Mindy. Since their arrival in Calvin, his half-sister had complained about every little thing. The townspeople were country bumpkins. The ranch house was too rustic and run-down after years of standing empty. The brother she hadn't met until six months ago was a stranger to her.

That one wasn't his fault.

Nathan's father had already been married when he'd had an affair with Nathan's mother. Neither had counted on a baby. In their tight-knit community in Pennsylvania, his mother had been ostracized not just by the townspeople but by her own family. Nate's father had only provided enough money for mother and son to move West, effectively abandoning them both. Mother had done the best she could, but she'd succumbed to a fever when Nate was sixteen. He'd had no choice but to join up with a large spread as a cowboy. He'd met Rob when he was eighteen, and Rob had done more than given him a job. He'd become a friend.

Nate had made a life for himself, simple as it was.

And then, six months ago, Mindy had arrived on Rob's doorstep with a letter and an inheritance Nate had never expected. Mindy's mother had passed years ago of a fever and her—their—father had died suddenly of an unknown heart problem. Apparently, his father *had* regretted leaving Nate with virtually nothing. He'd left everything to Nate until Mindy's twenty-first birthday, when she would receive a portion of the family fortune.

And she was very unhappy to be stuck with him. He didn't know how to reach her, didn't want to send her back to the women's finishing school in St. Louis.

He'd been alone for so long. He wanted to *know* her. He had a sister. The two of them were all they had left. They could be a family.

But it seemed she found him lacking as a brother.

"Watch your horse's footing," Rob cautioned. "Creek looks like it's flooding the banks. Danna mentioned it's been a dry season..."

They'd both worked out in the elements enough to know that dry ground would be packed to nearly solid, and if the rain had come on fast, it would run off more than soak in.

Nate reined in his mount. He hadn't even realized he'd come close to the creek's edge. "I apologize for my distraction."

He only had Rob for a few more days, a week at most, before the other man would return to his ranch up north. He should focus on his friend and not on his dark thoughts. Plus, today wasn't a day for distraction with a storm looming on the horizon. They'd already decided to ride for the ranch house, hoping to beat a soaking rain and dangerous lightning.

"I can't fault you for it," Rob said easily. "Miss Bennett *was* lovely last night."

Nate frowned. "I was thinking about a woman, but not that one. My sister."

"Ah." Rob nodded, squinting as he turned his face away.

"I don't suppose you have any advice to help ease my way with her."

Rob shook his head. "You know that sisters are not my expertise."

"Then perhaps I should pay more attention to our purpose today."

Rob chuckled and they rode on. They'd spent all morning and the early afternoon exploring the property, determining projects that would require Nate's immediate attention.

The land was beautiful. Everything Nate could've wanted, though he disliked the distance from Rob's spread, a day's ride by train or three on horseback.

How had he lucked into this? Except it wasn't luck at all. It was penance from the father who had never wanted him.

The fencing was in disrepair and the cattle were half-wild after being left on their own for over a year as the ranch sat vacant. The barn roof would perhaps last another year or two. But the stock horses were of good-quality.

He could be happy here.

"Is that...?"

He lifted his head at Rob's incredulous words, following the other man's stare.

"What?" And then he caught sight of the horse pulling itself from the creek.

It wore a saddle, now askew, and reins dangled loose from its bridle.

Where was its rider? Blood rushed through Nate's temples as he imagined a man lost to the swollen creek.

Rob kicked his mount with a quiet "hyah!" and Nate quickly followed.

On the opposite side of the creek a hundred yards upstream, a woman on horseback rode with her skirts flying like a flag. She was screaming something, but the roaring river and a booming clap of thunder made it impossible to hear.

He didn't rein in when he neared the riderless horse, but continued on toward the distraught woman. He didn't know how he and Rob might help from the opposite side of the creek, but—

He caught sight of the form in the creek at the same moment the shout from the woman on horseback reached his ears.

"Janie!"

Janie.

He didn't think past jumping from his horse. Still at a full gallop, his ankle jarred as he landed hard. He raced toward the creek bank and shucked his boots.

"Nate—"

Rob's shout rang from behind him, but he didn't stop.

He dove in, the icy waters an instant shock. The swirling current made it almost impossible to get his bearings, but he pushed to break the surface.

He'd gone in several yards behind Janie. With muddy water running into his eyes, it was impossible to see whether she was conscious, though he thought he glimpsed her face-down in the water.

No!

He kicked, using the current to push forward with more force. A log rammed into him, banging his shoulder and sending a grunt of pain from his lips.

He reached forward, grasping... *there*!

His fingers caught the back of her dress, and he clasped with all his might. Refused to let the water tear her from him. He scissored with his legs and finally managed to get an arm around her waist.

He hauled her to his chest, dread and fear rising when her head lolled against his shoulder.

Her body was limp and heavy. Her bulky skirts surrounded him, tangling both of their legs together.

For a moment, they were sucked beneath the surface.

He pushed hard, managing to kick free of the voluminous material. He had to get her out of it.

He fumbled, touching her waist in ways that weren't appropriate.

The water continued to push them downstream.

His fingers found the buttons at the back of her dress, and he managed to get two fingers between the tiny clasps, using what he could of his strength to rip the material.

Wet and slippery, it slipped through his fingers. The fabric remained as tight as ever. The situation was dire. He couldn't give up.

Finally, the material tore, giving way with one great rip, leaving her in an undershirt and petticoats. He let the current carry the dress away.

Without the weight of the material dragging them down, she was more buoyant in his arms. He saw blood smeared across her forehead. She was deathly pale, her lips blue and slightly open.

After being in the cold water for long minutes, his strength was waning.

They had to get out of the water, now.

Where was Rob?

Nate had no sense of direction, no idea where Rob might be, on horseback or on foot. No hope for a lasso to reach for.

He only knew that they couldn't stay in the water. He had to get Janie out.

A wave hit from behind, dunking Janie's head under again and resulting in Nate swallowing a mouthful of muddy water. He coughed and spluttered.

He turned downstream and saw a bend in the creek. A small jut of land ahead gave him hope. He struggled to both kick and keep Janie's head above the surface and managed to land hard against the muddy bank. The breath was knocked from his chest, and Janie began to slip from his arms.

And then Rob was there, pulling Janie's limp body from him and further up the bank.

Nate let himself inhale one shuddering breath. A great cough ripped through him. His legs felt as loose as molasses as he scrabbled up the bank to where Rob had laid Janie on a patch of dry grass.

One of her arms lay cocked at an unnatural angle. And she was so pale, so still. Had his rescue come too late?

On his knees beside the girl, Rob rolled her to the side and pounded on her back.

But she remained unmoving.

Liza had never ridden so fast. She'd lowered herself almost flat on Harvey's back, her cheek pressed to the horse's neck as she raced downstream. Tears streaked across her cheeks, the wind pulling them into her ears.

She cared not.

The creek widened just a little further downstream.

She'd seen Nathan Bingley pull Janie from the water, known that Rob Darcy was with him, on the opposite bank of the creek.

But Janie needed her sister.

This disaster would never have happened if Mama had listened to sense.

Was Janie dead? Drowned?

She couldn't think it.

The water was higher than she'd even imagined, because when she reached the field where the creek widened almost to a trickle on a normal day, the water spread out like a huge farm pond.

She didn't care.

She pushed the horse forward, its hooves splashing in the shallow water and sending droplets to wet her skirt, her hair, her face.

In the center of the creek, the water rose to the horse's flank, but Harvey didn't flounder, just pushed forward. Finally, they reached the other bank.

She gave another "hiyah!" and leaned low on the horse again.

The two men were silhouettes on the horizon. They came into view as she drew closer.

They were both bent over Janie, who lay unmoving on the ground. Her overskirt was gone, leaving only her underskirts and blouse. She was so still. Had Nathan's daring rescue come too late?

She reined in several yards away and jumped from the horse's back, fear making her legs wobble.

She couldn't give in to it. She picked up her skirts and rushed forward to see Mr. Darcy pounding on Janie's back, the movements almost violent, surely leaving bruises.

"Stop!" she cried, but he didn't even look her direction.

And then, just as she reached the little tableau, Janie coughed. A gurgle of water spilled from her lips and dribbled to the ground. Her eyes remained closed.

Rob pounded Janie's back again.

Another cough, this time a bigger one. Janie's eyes flew open, and she gagged, brown water vomiting from her mouth. She retched, her back bowing as Rob held her by the shoulders. Her lungs and stomach emptied their contents on the creek bank.

And then she was finished—a trembling, soaked, beautiful, *alive* sister.

"Janie!" Liza fell to her knees and reached for her. Janie looked as if she might collapse without Rob's hands at her shoulders.

"Careful," he said sharply, and Liza's gaze flew to his face. "Her shoulder."

Liza saw Janie's shoulder bone, which jutted out at an unnatural angle.

Rob reached out one hand toward Liza as if to catch her. Did he think she would faint from seeing her sister injured so?

She shot him a dark look and carefully gathered Janie close. Her sister was sobbing quietly.

Liza registered movement as Rob stood, moving away toward his horse. Two horses. His, and hers. She'd seen Nate abandon his horse upstream.

They needed to get Janie to the ranch house. Returning to town wasn't an option.

And then a guttural moan came from Mr. Bingley's direction, and Liza looked at him for the first time.

His face was almost as pale as Janie's had been, and his gaze hadn't left her sister. He appeared... devastated.

As if he already cared about Janie, at least a little bit.

"She needs care," Rob said, returning with his horse's reins. The animal followed him placidly, but Liza could see its spirit in its eyes, the bob of its head.

"If you'll help me boost her into the saddle," Liza said, "I'll ride with her to the ranch house."

Mr. Darcy shook his head, already handing off the reins to Mr. Bingley. "She's too weak, and I doubt you have the strength to support her for such a distance."

His highhandedness and assumptions mixed with the terror still coursing through her and sparked her temper. "You have no idea of my strength."

But Nathan had already swung into the saddle.

Liza looked at Janie, but her sister was silent, pale gray to match the angry sky. Rob reached for her, bodily removed her from Liza's arms, and lifted her to Nathan as if she weighed no more than a sack of flour. Janie couldn't contain a soft cry, and Liza felt an echo of her sister's pain slither down her spine.

Janie retched, leaning from the side of the horse, but Nathan held her fast. There was nothing left in her stomach, and the moment passed quickly.

Rob shrugged off his duster and tucked it around Janie, a moment that eased some of the sting of his past insults.

Nathan settled Janie with quiet words that Liza couldn't make out and turned the horse toward the Parrot ranch. He set out at a gallop.

"He'll jar her shoulder," Liza muttered as she whirled toward her horse.

"She was chilled from the water," Rob countered, keeping pace at her side. Drat his long legs. "Best to get her warmed up as quickly as possible."

She shot a look at him. What did he know about Janie's needs? Liza was her sister.

However, his worry over Janie's well-being negated some of her temper over his highhandedness.

Some. Not all.

When she reached her horse, she didn't hesitate to put her foot in the stirrup and swing up into the saddle. She adjusted her skirts, flushing a little at the idea that Rob had seen her ankles, but it couldn't be helped.

He stood close, his Stetson knocked back slightly on his forehead, which made it that much easier to see the raise of his brows.

"You aren't thinking of leaving me on foot out here?"

She couldn't help the smile that crossed her lips at the thought. It would serve him right after his insulting comment about her last night. She shrugged, affecting the most innocent mien she could muster. "Mr. Bingley's horse was left behind, wasn't it...?"

His brows formed a line that any thunderhead would be proud of.

"And while Janie's injury makes it necessary for her to ride with Mr. Bingley, it wouldn't be proper for us to ride together."

Now his face was a mask of temper. "Proper?" She saw his lips move, forming the word, but a clap of thunder crashed overhead and stole his voice.

Her horse danced sideways, and it was all she could do to keep control. How humiliating it would be to lose her seat in front of Rob Darcy!

She'd only meant to tease him, had intended to laugh at his consternation, but, "Never mind," she said. "This is no time for joshing. Come on." She moved her left foot out of the stirrup temporarily and motioned for him to join her in the saddle.

He reached for the saddle horn and his fingers tangled with hers momentarily.

Still on the ground, his gaze flew to her face. What was he thinking behind those eyes? She saw something, but it couldn't be admiration, could it? Not after last night... And she was sure her hair had slipped in its pins and hung in a sodden mess after this afternoon's wild ride.

She jerked her hand away, and he gripped the saddle horn.

The saddle shifted slightly beneath his weight, and then he settled behind her, his long legs framing her hips, the heat of his body searing her.

Heat flamed in her face, and she sat as straight in the saddle as she possibly could.

She'd been right. This wasn't proper at all.

Rob let his hands rest at Liza Bennett's waist only because there was nothing else to hold on to.

Yeah, that was it.

He didn't know what to do with a woman like Liza Bennett.

She'd been... teasing him. Pretending that she'd leave him on foot. He had the sense that if the coming storm hadn't frightened her horse—and the woman herself?—she'd have laughed that pealing, bell-like laugh that had haunted his dreams.

No one else in his life dared tease him.

Not even Danna.

"Where'd you cross the creek?" he shouted, because he wasn't sure she'd hear him over the rushing wind in her ears or the pounding of the horse's hooves as they galloped.

"The land turns flat another half mile downstream," she said over her shoulder, giving him a view of the apple of her cheek and the dark sweep of her lashes against her skin.

She'd been intelligent enough to know she had to find a shallow crossing or risk getting swept away like her sister had. How had Janie come to be in the creek anyway?

"The bridge washed out while Janie was crossing," Liza said, as if she'd sensed where his thoughts had gone.

"Were you with her?" He imagined Liza being the one in the water, her face as pale as death, and those thoughts sent a ripple of terror right through him.

She shook her head.

He worried for Janie. Her shoulder had obviously been dislocated. But the real danger was the chill she'd have from being in the cold water for so long.

Nate knew that. He would take care of Janie. She couldn't have found a better protector.

Which left Rob with Liza. Much too close.

She pointed. There was Nate's abandoned horse, trotting through the field toward a tree line. In the trees, Rob could just make out what must be Janie's horse, huddling in the scrub trees for shelter.

Liza headed that direction.

She was a good horsewoman. Was that why she'd managed to avoid being swept downriver?

She reined in and he whistled for Nate's horse as he dismounted from Liza's. He kept one hand on the pommel to keep her from immediately galloping off.

He had to know. "What kept you from falling in the creek?"

The sweep of her lashes hid her gaze from him. But twin roses of color appeared in her fair cheeks. "I was following Janie secretly. She's not the strongest rider, and I wanted to make sure she arrived for her visit with Mindy. Mama insisted she ride…"

Something about the way her mouth snapped closed over the words and the slant of her gaze away from his brought reality intruding back. Her mother had been involved in today's disaster somehow. She couldn't have wanted Janie to be injured, but... if Janie wasn't a strong rider, why send her on horseback at all?

Liza shifted in the saddle, and her horse reacted, breaking Rob's hold.

"I must go to Janie. Fetch our mare, will you?" she called the words over her shoulder as she rode away.

He watched her, a frown blooming on his face.

Of course he would retrieve the animal, but not because of her presumptuous demand. A horse was valuable, and he'd hate for her father to lose the animal.

That was all.

And then he would send the two women home where they belonged.

5

Janie forced herself to remain upright on the horse, barely able to think through the haze of pain. It throbbed from her shoulder outward. Another point radiated from her lower back. Perhaps she'd wrenched something there as well?

Her throat burned, and every breath she drew made her chest ache.

But she was alive. Thank the Lord for that.

Tears welled and she sniffed. The quick intake of air burned all the way down.

"I'm sorry," Nathan murmured. "I know it's a rough ride." His arm tightened around her waist.

The horse shifted, and her shoulder twinged in pain. She held back a gasp.

She was trying to ignore the fact that she was pressed up against him in nothing but a shirtwaist, petticoats, and Rob's coat. The heat emanating from Nathan fought against the chill that slithered down her arms and made gooseflesh prick her skin.

"Th-thank you for coming in after me." She'd blacked out

beneath the water, nearly drowned. When she'd come to, coughing and retching, she'd immediately seen Nathan soaked to the skin and known what he'd done.

His chin pressed against her temple. Purposely?

"How could I not?" he murmured.

A cough rattled her chest and jarred her shoulder. This time she couldn't contain the gasp of pain.

She closed her eyes. Maybe she drifted off. She lost all sense of time passing. And then she was awake and aware of the man behind her again.

What must Nathan think of her? Humiliation washed over her in a wave of heat that left her shivering in the cool wind.

Nathan had seen her in a completely improper state of dress. Was holding her close, no chaperone in sight. Liza had been nearby, hadn't she?

What if someone from town found out about this?

What if Mama found out? She couldn't fathom the disaster *that* would be. Mama would demand an engagement to save Janie's reputation.

This couldn't be happening again. The very last thing she wanted was to bring more humiliation to her family. Or to herself.

She must find a way to limit the damage.

Another cough wracked her, and this time the pain became so intense, she fainted.

NATHAN REINED in his horse just outside the barn. He roused Janie from where she'd either fainted or drifted off in his arms. He bade her sit still while he slid from the horse and reached for her. She was white-faced and bit her lip in pain, though he tried not to jostle her.

He sent the horse into the barn with a swat on its rump and

headed to the house. The sky unleashed a torrent of rain as his boots hit the porch stair.

He banged through the door. The kitchen was dark, shadowed. Was the stove even lit?

"Mindy!" he roared.

His sister's head appeared from the parlor doorway. "What?" she snapped. Her eyes widened when she caught sight of Janie in his arms.

"I need your help. She was swept away in the creek. Her shoulder is out of socket."

Mindy backed away, hands up in front of her. "What do you want me to do? I don't know anything about... about anything."

He stuffed his anger. Mindy had let the kitchen fire die, there wasn't a stitch of supper in sight, and she was reluctant to help.

None of those complaints needing voicing. Janie was more important right now.

"Get some blankets. Bring them upstairs to the corner bedroom. We need to fix her shoulder."

Mindy shook her head. "No!"

His temper surged. The muscles in his arms began to protest against Janie's weight. No surprise after the ordeal he'd gone through to fish her out of the flooded creek.

Surely Rob was right behind him. And Janie's sister. He needed help. Janie needed help.

He gave one more attempt. "Mindy, on a ranch, everyone must pitch in and do what's needed."

Mindy's eyes flashed. "I don't *want* to be on your ranch!"

She ran up the stairs ahead of him, leaving him to carry Janie up alone and settle her in the bedroom. She stirred as he laid her flat on the bed and he moved back, aware that propriety was already out the window but unsure whether he should wait—

There! Hoofbeats sounded from the yard below. He flicked back the curtain to see Liza gallop to the barn and jump off her horse.

Thank God.

Rob was soaked by the time he reached Nathan's barn. The rain had started a good quarter hour ago, and with Janie Bennett wearing his coat, he'd had no protection from the stinging water.

Judging by the state of her horse, she'd arrived at the barn not long before him. She was nowhere to be seen, but her horse stood in an open stall, still saddled. Nathan's wandered free in the barn itself, also saddled. The abundance of storm clouds made it so dark in the barn that Rob could hardly see.

The animals were lathered with sweat. He could only hope Janie had benefited from their rush.

He unsaddled and put away the horses, promising himself to return after he'd checked on Janie and give them the brushing they deserved. For now, this would have to do.

Rivulets of water ran across the hard-packed dirt as he crossed the yard toward the house. His boots splashed through them.

Safely in the kitchen, he took off his Stetson and boots before reaching for the kitchen towel. A lit lamp sat on the table, casting shadows in the near-dark.

He desperately wanted a cup of coffee, but the stove in the corner of the room wasn't putting off any heat. Mindy. He bit back a snarl of frustration. The girl was spoiled and high strung, and Rob wished Nate luck with her. Rob wouldn't miss her at all when he returned home.

He was mopping his face and neck with the towel when the soft swish of a skirt alerted him to the presence of another.

Liza swept into the room, just her presence sending electric charges through the air as if lightning were about to strike. Her clothing appeared damp. She carried an armful of wood against her midsection and stopped short.

"Good, you're here," she said.

She knelt in front of the stove and opened its door, sending him a glance. Her focus caught on his chest, and he realized that his soaked shirt clung to his skin. Her gaze skittered away, and he felt a moment of male satisfaction. She found his form pleasing.

Her load of wood fell to the floor with a clatter.

He eyed the empty wood box just behind the stove. Liza shot a much shorter glance at him this time. "I raided the firebox in the parlor."

The ranch house had been built for entertaining, with one great room and a huge rock fireplace that had surely cost a pretty penny. They hadn't lit it earlier, as the day had been warm.

And somehow, Mindy had let the kitchen fire go out. "I'll refill the box," he said. "There's a rick of wood outside."

She nodded and set about crumpling a page of newsprint from the bottom of the wood box and arranging some kindling with it in the belly of the stove. Her movements were economical and efficient.

He moved across the room, his wet clothes chafing with every step. Coffee. This entire situation called for coffee. He found the pot on a high shelf above the kitchen work counter and a pitcher of water and then reached to the shelf for the coffee beans.

When she spoke, her voice was slightly muffled as she worked on her task. "With the creek already swollen and the bridge gone and now more rains... it would take too long to fetch the doctor. If he's even in town tonight." She reached for the flint and tinder in the bottom of the box.

He'd expected as much.

"Nathan seems..." Her voice trailed off, worried. "I'm not sure he'll be able to assist with Janie's arm."

"Nathan will do what's needed."

There was a scrape and a *whoosh* as her paper ignited. The soft flare of light in the room limned her features with gold and threw shadows in her eyes when she looked up at him.

"He seems very concerned for her," Liza agreed. "But her arm needs to be set, and I'm not certain he'll be able to cause her pain." A small smile played about her lips, as if she knew something he didn't.

As if she suspected his friend was sweet on her sister.

Nathan's preoccupation with the young woman hadn't gone unnoticed, but he hadn't seemed to want to talk about her as they'd ridden today.

Rob firmed his lips in a line.

Her eyes scanned his face and the hint of merriment in her gaze was quickly banked. She turned back to the task of feeding wood into the flame and within minutes, had a hardy fire crackling.

"According to Mr. Bingley, his sister suffered a fit of vapors when he and Janie arrived."

He'd just bet. So Mindy would be of no use to them. She'd probably barricaded herself in her room.

Liza closed the stove door and stood, touching the back of one wrist to her forehead. She must be exhausted, too, after a wild ride in the approaching storm and rushing to her sister's aide. The droop of her shoulders made him want to reach for her. Offer comfort or... hold her.

He flexed his hands at his sides to keep from doing so. Where had the errant impulse come from?

"I'll help with setting Janie's arm," he said.

Liza didn't look him in the eye again. "Thank you," she murmured to the floor.

"Just let me put a pot of coffee on," he said, "and I'll follow you up."

She left the room, and he heard her tread on the stair.

The strange urge to offer comfort remained, even after her departure, though he refused to act on it. There was something about him that made her natural smile disappear. Probably the insult he'd slung so casually. Had it only been yesterday?

He should apologize. Probably.

But her sister's care came first.

6

Liza woke to a weak, rattling cough from her sister, who lay beside her.

"Janie?" She rolled over to face her, the quilt tangling around her legs. The room where Nathan had settled Janie must have been meant for the master of the house. The feather-tick was large enough for the both of them. Janie was curled into a ball beneath the quilt, shivering despite the blanket.

"I'm all right."

But the wheeze of Janie's breath belied her whisper.

"You aren't."

Without a light to see whether Janie's cheeks were flushed, she reached out and touched Janie's forehead. Her skin was dry and hot.

"You've got a fever. Are you chilled?"

"I can't tell a difference from earlier. I've been so cold since the cr-creek."

"How's your shoulder?"

"Aches."

Liza could only imagine that was an understatement. Rob

had been as good as his word, appearing minutes after Liza had come upstairs. He'd changed into a dry shirt, which had hung untucked over pants still a shade dark with dampness. Janie had been stoic while Rob and Liza had manipulated her shoulder back into its socket, but she hadn't been able to hold back a scream of pain when it finally popped.

Nathan had had to leave the room. That he was unable to witness Janie in pain intrigued Liza, but there hadn't been time to dwell on it. She would revisit it when Janie was better.

Janie had allowed herself to be plied with willow bark tea and claimed exhaustion. After her ordeal, Liza hadn't challenged her need for rest.

But now Janie's labored breathing was worrisome. Had the water Janie ingested injured her lungs somehow?

"I'm going to make a plaster." Liza sat up and swung her legs to the side of the bed.

"No." Janie grabbed her chemise, but Liza knew a moment of fear at the weakness of her sister's grip. "You'll wake everyone."

Liza didn't care. "I'll be quiet."

Janie's grip shifted to Liza's wrist. Her voice was insistent. "There mustn't be a hint of impropriety, Liza. Not a hint!" Janie's voice shook.

Was her worry for the Bingleys? Or because of what had happened in Cottonwood Cove? Liza could guess.

She didn't want Janie getting more upset. "All right. I promise. See, I'm getting dressed."

She slipped her dress over her underclothes and buttoned up. She hadn't been willing to disturb the sensitive Mindy for another nightgown after the girl had disappeared into her room. She didn't bother with shoes and padded barefoot out of the room after sweeping her fingers across Janie's forehead once more. She kept one hand on the wall as she crept down the darkened hall, not comfortable with the unfamiliar surroundings.

In the kitchen, the stove was still warm. Someone must've banked the fire. The storm had cleared, and moonlight filtered through the window, though thin clouds blocked some of it.

Liza opened the stove door and soft, orange light burnished the room. She easily found the tin canister of flour and the water pitcher, but where was the mustard? The ranch house had been vacant for so long... had Nathan and Mindy replenished the kitchen necessities?

She rifled through the contents of the cabinet as quietly as she could. Was it... there. She opened a small jar and sniffed its contents. Ground mustard.

She'd set her supplies on the counter and turned back to find a pot when a dark figure appeared in the doorway. She startled and stepped back, her hands clutching the counter behind her.

"Everything all right?"

Rob.

Her breath left her in one big whoosh, and she raised one hand to press against her chest, where her heart pounded.

He stepped into the room. In the light thrown by the stove, she saw his feet were bare as well. For some reason, that sight sent a hot flush through her.

She hated feeling weak in front of him, and her words emerged with a sharp edge, though she spoke softly. "Janie's come down with a cough."

"The water in her lungs?"

She nodded, returning to her task. Maybe he would simply go back to bed.

She added water to a pot and began to heat it on the stove, mixing in flour and mustard.

"Here."

Surprised to find him at her elbow, she jumped again.

"Sorry." He held out a fold of white cloth. "These are old—from the previous owner. You can use them."

Linens. Because she'd mixed the paste she'd need for Janie's plaster, but she'd completely forgotten about linens to make the wrap. Being woken in the darkest hours of night made her thoughts slower.

Their hands brushed when he handed her the pile of cloths. The intimacy of the moment couldn't be ignored—the neck of his shirt was open, and though it was shadowed, she could see the planes of his upper chest and a darker shadow of hair that disappeared beneath the shirt.

She felt both breathless and lightheaded, the same way she had when she'd first glimpsed him across the crowd of dancers.

But Janie was suffering upstairs.

She turned away and set the fabric on the counter. She cleared her throat. "Thank you." Her voice trembled with the force of the emotions ricocheting through her body. Her hands trembled as she unfolded the fabric and began to tear it into long strips.

"Do you require anything else?" *His* voice was steady. Had the moment left him completely unaffected?

"No. You can return to your bed. I'm sorry that we've disturbed you and the Bingleys."

She left him standing in the kitchen and climbed the stairs to Janie, but even after she'd applied the plaster and Janie had fallen back into a restless sleep, Liza remained awake, staring into the darkness.

Why did Rob affect her so strongly? Even before he'd insulted her, she'd felt an instant pull toward the man.

Not that it mattered.

Janie was her priority. The sooner they could return home, the better. She could only pray that Janie's cough wasn't serious. With the bridge out, it was a long, dangerous ride to fetch the town doctor.

Janie's insistence on maintaining propriety was a much-needed reminder to Liza of her place. She was the reason for Janie's broken heart, the reason their family had been uprooted.

Papa's store was in dire straits, and Liza would fix that too.

She didn't have time for romance, for silly imaginings. Rob was standoffish and highhanded. He wasn't interested in her. And he was leaving in a matter of days.

Better for her to concentrate on seeing Janie healed and smoothing things over with Nathan Bingley.

JANIE ROLLED her head across the pillow before cracking her eyes open. Her neck was so stiff. Why—?

Memories of her freefall into the murky creek and the terror of being unable to swim to the surface rushed over her, much like the raging waters had done. She gasped.

Her throat and lungs burned. Her chest felt like a heavy weight was pressed on her. Heavier than Mama's old, fat tomcat.

A candle had been lit on the beside table, and its small flame lit the corner of the room. The curtains were drawn, but no light peeked around their edges. What time was it? Was it still the middle of the night?

"Liza?" she whispered. She'd gone in and out of restless sleep, but hadn't her sister been here moments ago?

Someone stirred, and she turned her head on the pillow.

It wasn't Liza sitting in the wooden chair at her bedside. It was Nathan.

His hair was sleep-tousled, and his shirt was rumpled and buttoned askew—one button was off, at the very top. He was so dear, but she was intensely aware of the nightgown she wore beneath the quilt. It was highly improper for him to be here. And that made her think of Albert. And Edna. And the lies she'd told about Janie.

He poured water from a pitcher on the dresser, sat beside her again, and lifted the cup to her lips.

The heat of his hand seared her cheek as he cupped her face and helped her sip the cool water. Or maybe that was the blush that felt like a raging brush fire across her skin.

"Mr. Bingley—"

He smiled, and her stomach flip-flopped. "I think, after what we've been through together, you'd better call me Nathan."

Nathan.

She swallowed with some difficulty, her face still feeling like a glowing firebrand. Perhaps the candlelight was such that he couldn't see her blush. She could only hope.

"Where's my sister?" she whispered.

"She was up with you most of the night, changing out your plasters in the hopes of easing your breathing."

She remembered that. Some of it, anyway. The sharp scent of the mustard and the warmth of the plaster against her chest. Was that the weight she felt now, or was it inside her lungs?

"I offered to relieve her and sent her to bed with Mindy. She was wobbling on her feet. It's almost dawn now."

That was kind of him. But what had he been doing awake at such an hour?

"I... couldn't sleep," he admitted, as if he'd followed the direction of her thoughts. "I couldn't live with myself if something happened to you."

What a thing to say. She'd felt a connection with him from their first dance, but...

He rushed on. "If I had pulled you from the creek more quickly, maybe you wouldn't be suffering now."

She touched his wrist. It was presumptuous, and instantly she heard echoes of Albert's mother screaming about propriety. But Nathan had sounded so anguished that she hadn't been able to stop herself.

"I would've drowned if not for you."

He clasped her fingers tightly. "I'm happy to have been of service. I just wish..."

There was something there, in the clasp of his hands, in the depths of his gaze. But she was so sleepy and her chest ached so very badly.

"Sleep," he said quietly. "We've time to talk in the morning."

She meant to ask him to leave, to insist they keep a proper distance, but sleep claimed her again.

7

I'm sorry that we've disturbed you.

Liza Bennett's words rolled around in Rob's head like the marbles he'd played with as a boy.

She couldn't know how deeply her presence had affected him. It made no sense. He'd only known the woman two days.

From the moment he'd seen her, he hadn't been able to get her out of his head.

Even now, as he washed up in the kitchen after a morning spent doing chores in the barn, he listened for her tread on the stair or in the parlor. She was probably still sleeping, given how often she'd been up in the night caring for her sister. Her devotion was something to admire, something rare. Nate had mentioned in passing that he'd practically had to pry her from Janie's bedside even though she'd been incoherent with exhaustion.

And seeing her in the moonlight, her hair down around her shoulders and her face sleep-soft... It had affected him more than he wanted to admit.

A sharp knock sounded, and he whirled. He'd been so lost in his thoughts he hadn't noticed a rider?

He opened the door and found his sister on the stoop. Behind her, storm clouds built on the horizon. The air was humid and expectant.

"Danna!"

She didn't wait for an invitation but moved right into his arms for a hug, and he spared a moment to send a prayer of thanks heavenward. Two years ago, he'd been out of communication with her with no hope of that changing. Then she'd nearly died when she'd been abducted by a gang of horse thieves, and he'd promised himself he'd fix their relationship, whatever it took.

"What're you doing out this way?" he asked.

She moved out of his arms, followed him when he motioned her inside. He went straight to the coffeepot, and she nodded.

"For one, I came to find out why my brother would attend a town dance but not make time for a visit to his only, beloved sister."

He had to snort at her obviously overblown statement. Danna was the least womanly woman he'd ever met. She didn't get her feelings hurt over trivial matters.

"The dance was Nathan's doing."

She winked as he handed her the coffee mug. "I imagined as much."

She was the one who'd suggested Nathan look into the Parrott's old ranch in the first place. She knew the area, and she'd grown up on their parents' ranch, so she knew what was needed to raise cattle and crops. Having both her and Nathan in Calvin would give him ample excuses to visit them both.

She sipped her coffee. "I'm scouting for a pair of lost young women. One of them was supposed to visit here yesterday, but neither returned home last night. Their parents are understandably worried."

"They're here," Rob said.

Danna's brows rose slightly. "I saw the bridge washed out. Had to ride almost a mile out of the way to find a crossing."

"Janie Bennett was on the bridge when it was swept away."

"What?" Her cup clattered to the counter. "Is she—?"

"Nathan fished her out of the creek. Those heavy skirts…" He shook his head, remembering how Janie's head had slipped beneath the water. "She nearly drowned."

Danna shook her head. She often wore trousers in her job as town marshal, but she'd worn enough skirts to understand the danger.

"We roused her, but she'd dislocated one shoulder and taken in quite a bit of water. She started feverin' in the night. Liza sat up with her all night. Doing mustard plasters."

"Liza?" Danna cast a curious gaze.

He turned away, conflicted in his feelings for the pretty Liza and not wanting Danna to see. His sister was sharper than a newly-forged blade.

He rubbed the back of his neck, heat flaring there. "She was following her sister, and after Janie's rescue, she insisted on staying here. Both horses are in the barn. Fed and sheltered."

"Of course," Danna murmured.

His sister wasn't a murmurer, and he turned a sharp gaze on her. Her eyes were wide and innocent—and she must have some techniques for making a suspect talk, because he found himself wanting to spill all his muddled feelings.

He clamped his lips closed instead.

"With the bridge out and another storm on the horizon," he said instead, "we can't exactly load the pair of them in a wagon and take them to town."

"Hmm." That suspicious sound carried through a couple of ticks of the grandfather clock before she continued. "I'll take the news back, let their Mama know they'll be delivered when the creek subsides."

He nodded.

"Flash flooding usually only lasts a day or two around here," she said.

He nodded again.

It was she who broke first. "Oh, Rob. Is Nathan very interested in Janie Bennett? Her mama told me that he'd danced with her five times and that Janie is the best catch in Calvin—something she tells *everyone* who comes in her shop."

Not surprising, given what he'd heard that first day in town.

Rob shrugged. He had some idea how Nate felt, but that was his friend's business. "She's barely been conscious."

Danna fiddled with her cup. "Just tell him to be careful. If anyone can snare a man, it's Maude Bennett."

Her words were a douse of icy water. She'd touched on the one thing that would be a sore point for Nate. And Rob needed to remember what his friend had been through. Protect Nate, if possible. It's what he'd come down for.

"And what of you?" Danna asked. "Have you been caught by Janie's pretty sister?" Her laugh seemed to indicate she thought it highly unlikely.

He might've been insulted, if she didn't know him so well.

"I'm a confirmed bachelor. Much more difficult to catch than the jovial Nathan." But for the first time, the words left a bitter taste in his mouth.

"Yes, I remember."

And her teasing only made him conscious of the reason she'd left him to marry Fred Carpenter at sixteen. She'd nearly died because of Rob.

He wasn't gentle enough for a woman. Didn't mince words, didn't know how to give them the softness they needed. He couldn't coddle someone when there were numerous jobs to keep the spread running, keep the animals healthy and put food on the table.

Danna looked around. "Maybe it's just as well. I'm not sure those town gals would enjoy living on a ranch, anyway. It's isolated and probably more work than they're used to at their father's shop."

She was right. Of course she was. His ranch—and Nathan's—were no place for either of the pretty Bennett daughters.

LIZA WOKE to the crow of a rooster, but upon glancing out the window, the reddish cast to the sky confused her. It must be mid-morning, but another storm was brewing on the horizon, the clouds giving the sky a strange hue.

Mindy was nowhere to be seen. The girl had only rolled over with a mumble when Liza had climbed into bed a couple of hours before dawn, after Nathan had sent her away from Janie's bedside.

With a few hours of rest, she could see he'd been right. She'd been so exhausted she might've set the house on fire if she'd tried to make one more plaster.

She needed to check on Janie.

She splashed her face in the water basin and did what she could with her hair. She'd left her pins in Janie's room, so she made a simple braid down her back and tied it off with a snippet of ribbon she'd left in her dress pocket. Were Mama and Papa worried for them? Had a search party been sent from town? With the creek flooded, it would be a long ride for anyone who came after them.

The looking glass above the dresser showed weary lines around her eyes. Her rumpled, creek-stained dress desperately needed a wash and iron, but there was no help for it now. She attempted to pinch some color into her cheeks and went in search of her sister.

From the hallway, she cracked Janie's door to find her sister sleeping and Nathan absent. Liza didn't go in, didn't want to disturb her. She listened in the doorway for a long time. Janie seemed to be breathing easier, and Liza had to blink back tears of relief. She would apply another plaster when her sister woke and hope that the mustard paste would draw the last of the muddy water from Janie's lungs.

How would they get home? Even if the creek had subsided, another storm was on the way. Surely they couldn't rely on the Bingleys' hospitality much longer.

Downstairs, she found Mindy curled in the corner of the settee, reading.

Liza wrinkled her nose. The girl was useless, but *someone* was cooking. She smelled... biscuits? And ham, if she wasn't mistaken.

Mindy was plenty old enough to be preparing a meal. But if she was in here, who was in the kitchen?

She entered and found Rob at the stove. He was in his sock feet, as if he were at home. His sleeves were rolled up, revealing muscled forearms, and he'd tossed a towel over his shoulder. He was using a fork to stir roux in a cast iron pan. Platters on the counter beside him were loaded with biscuits and ham. It sat alongside a bowl heaped with scrambled eggs.

He glanced at her briefly. "Good, you're awake. It's more lunch than breakfast, but it'll be ready in a few minutes."

She stood and stared.

"You... cooked?"

He shot a wry smile over his shoulder. "I've been a bachelor a very long time. Plus, you wouldn't have wanted to eat Mindy's food."

Liza heard a pouty sniff from the parlor behind her, but

when she glanced over her shoulder, Mindy still had her nose buried in her book.

Nathan banged in the kitchen door and hung his hat on a peg. "Smells good, old man." He caught sight of Liza as he headed for the wash basin. "Mornin'."

"Good morning. Thank you for sitting with Janie. I peeked in on her, and she seems to be breathing easier."

Nathan nodded, and open relief crossed his face before he bent to douse it with water.

Rob reached for a bowl on the counter, probably ready to pour out the gravy that smelled so good her mouth was watering.

"I'll take these." Liza reached for the eggs and the platter of ham and carried them to the dining table.

Mindy roused herself to come and sit at the table, though there were still table settings to be made.

Liza couldn't help the raise of her brows as she returned to the kitchen.

Rob noticed, and a smile twitched his lips. "Don't ask," he whispered.

Nathan's head turned from where he was taking down plates from an upper cabinet.

She went to him and held out both hands. "What am I not supposed to ask about?"

Nathan placed two plates in her hands and reached for a third. "Mindy."

"Ah."

"I just want to go back to finishing school," Mindy said petulantly from the table.

"They don't teach setting a table at that kind of school?" Liza asked. She couldn't help it.

Nathan winked as he stacked forks and knives on top of the plates Liza held. "Not for setting a *ranch* table."

Liza took the plates and silverware to the table and began setting each place. Rob brought the bowl of gravy and the plate of biscuits to the table, and it seemed almost natural to duck around him as she moved to the next place. A dance, almost, like the one he hadn't asked her for.

It discomfited her, and she looked for a quick distraction. "You don't like the ranch?" she asked Mindy.

"I prefer the city," the young woman said stiffly. "When my parents died, I was forced to leave my friends, my life behind. I invited your sister to tea because I thought she'd provide some bearable company. And see how well that's turned out."

Liza would've taken offense at Mindy's bitter words about Janie, but she couldn't help feeling compassion for such an ordeal. Not that it was an excuse for Mindy's behavior.

"I'm sorry for your loss," she said.

Nathan joined them at the table, his mouth tight. He'd lost his family, too. She couldn't help reaching out to touch his arm. "And yours."

A muscle ticked in his jaw. "I lost my mother when I was sixteen."

But Mindy had said—

"I never met my father."

Oh.

Across the table, Rob sat, silent and serious.

Mindy's face crumpled. "You shouldn't punish *me* because of what Papa did to you!"

In the shocked silence that followed her outburst, Mindy ran from the room and up the stairs. Moments later, her bedroom door slammed, the sound reverberating through the house.

"I told you not to ask." Rob reached for a biscuit, splitting it and adding both pieces to his plate.

"I'm sorry," Nathan said. "Please excuse my sister's behavior."

"*I'm* sorry that I touched a nerve," she said. "I didn't realize..." With all the gossip in town about the Bingleys, Nathan's parentage hadn't come up once. Not that it was anyone's business but his own.

Nathan kept his focus on his own plate. "It has been a difficult six months. With Mindy."

"No doubt. My own sisters, my younger sisters, often drive me to distraction."

His head came up, and she smiled at him. "It can't last forever, can it?" she asked.

He returned her smile. "Let's hope not."

She didn't dare look at Rob, but she felt his stare anyway.

8

Knock, knock.

Liza must've dozed off in the chair beside Janie's bed. She roused now as Nathan's head popped in the door.

Janie was sitting up in bed, and twin roses of color appeared on her cheeks. She carefully smoothed the quilt over her legs.

"How is our patient, nurse?" he teased Liza.

"Her cough is a little better, I think."

Janie brushed at a few strands of hair that had come loose from the braid down her back. "Liza's plasters have worked miracles. I'm much improved, Mr.—I-I mean, Nathan. Ready to go home."

"We can't—"

"There's a storm—"

Liza and Nathan spoke at the same time, both cut off by a rumble of thunder.

"I rode out to the creek this morning, and it's still too high to haul a wagon across," Nathan said. "If the storm today brings more rain, you may be stuck with my company for another day or two. Such that it is."

"Your company is fine," Janie said softly. "Very fine."

Nathan lit up, though Janie was looking down at her lap and didn't see it.

"I brought something to help you pass the time." He stepped into the room and offered Janie a hard-bound book.

She took it, mumbling her thanks to her lap. He watched her for a long moment and then took his leave.

Just yesterday morning, Janie had been lost in daydreams—Liza had thought those daydreams were about Nathan. But today she picked at the quilt, her discomfort obvious.

Was she embarrassed? Or had her feelings for Nathan changed?

"That was kind," Liza said carefully.

"Mm-hmm."

Liza was used to Janie's shyness, but her sister's attitude this morning was something... more than that.

"Perhaps this evening you'll feel up to joining the Bingleys for supper. It would be a shame to be stuck out here and not get to know Nathan better."

After discovering that he'd taken in his sister and witnessing his patience with the recalcitrant teen firsthand, Liza was more certain than ever that Nathan was an upstanding man. He could be a good match for the tender-hearted Janie.

Janie ran one finger over the cover of the book in her lap. "You sound like Mama."

Liza wrinkled her nose. "Never." She stood and moved to the window, flicking the curtain. The storm hadn't broken yet, though wind buffeted the house. Clouds rolled through the sickly gray sky. "If you're worried that Nathan is like Albert, he—"

Janie gasped slightly, cutting her off. "Liza. Your hands."

She looked down, saw what Janie had seen. Flexed her

fingers, which were chapped and red from repeating the mustard plasters.

"It's nothing." Janie's health was worth the discomfort.

A streak of lightning split the sky with white, making Liza blink against the temporary blindness. Thunder shook the house.

That had been close.

Janie fidgeted beneath her blanket. "I don't wish to talk about Albert. Ever."

Liza knew he'd betrayed Janie and broken her heart, but that didn't mean Janie should keep her heart shut away.

Earlier they'd cracked the window to allow in a breath of cool air, and now Liza scented the barest hint of smoke.

Had the house been hit by lightning? Urgency surged, her heart pounding against her breastbone. She couldn't see anything amiss from here, just fields dotted with cattle.

But the smell didn't dissipate. Something had caught fire. Was it the other side of the house? A tree?

She sent a glance to Janie and decided she couldn't risk it. "We must go downstairs. I smell smoke."

Janie gestured to the nightgown and wrap she wore. "I can't go down like this."

"If the house is on fire, there's no time to dress."

Janie protested again, but Liza cut her off. "Downstairs. Now."

Janie was slow on the stairs, once dissolving into a fit of coughing, and Liza had to bite back words when she would rush her.

They crossed toward the parlor, and out this window, Liza had a view of the barn. Where a curl of smoke rose from the roof.

"The barn's on fire."

Mindy looked up from a needlework project she was poring over.

Janie let out a small gasp. "Oh, no."

The men were nowhere in sight. Already outside?

Liza turned her most serious look on her sister. She pointed a finger at the sofa. "Sit down and stay here. Your lungs cannot do battle with smoke today."

Janie looked torn, but Liza narrowed her eyes, and her sister perched on the edge of the sofa.

Next Liza pointed her finger at Mindy. "Come with me."

The girl let out a squeak of what might be protest. But there was no time for arguing, so Liza grasped her arm and pulled her to her feet.

Mindy might be a spoiled city girl, but Nathan needed help. Now.

"If the barn is destroyed, your brother will lose his stock and supplies for the winter. You *must* help." She dragged the girl across the threshold and out onto the porch.

The scent of smoke was stronger outdoors. She caught sight of Rob rounding the barn just before he disappeared from sight. Nate was heading into the barn through open double doors.

"The grass is still damp from yesterday's rain," she said for Mindy's benefit. "But if the hay in the barn catches fire, the entire structure could be lost."

Mindy was wide-eyed, but there wasn't time for her hysterics.

"You don't have to go near the fire," she told the other girl. "But you can pump water."

She tucked her arm through the crook of Mindy's elbow. If they had been friends, attending a tea or dance, the move would have felt entirely natural. The fire made it necessary.

"What about the neighbors?" Mindy cried.

"They won't make it in time."

She dragged Mindy to the horse trough and shoved her toward the pump handle. Mindy looked at her askance, and Liza primed it and got the first gushes of water flowing.

"Don't stop," she told the girl.

Buckets.

When she turned to the barn, Nate was already running toward the trough, his arms full of feed buckets.

"The horses," he gasped as she passed.

She ran into the barn, where smoke was beginning to curl beneath the loft, thick enough to send her into a coughing spasm. A crackling sound and intense heat from overhead meant it was likely too late to save the hay. Was it too late for the structure as well?

In the stalls, six or seven horses paced and turned, including Buckles and Harvey, Janie and Liza's mounts. They were all agitated. One whinnied, the sound an echo of the panic rising in Liza.

She moved to the first stall and lugged away the two heavy boards that blocked the horse from escaping. As soon as it could, the horse bolted, hooves pounding against the packed dirt floor before it fled outside.

She let two more horses out before a coughing fit made her bend at the waist. Precious seconds were lost while she caught her breath. Each inhale was laborious.

A man appeared in the doorway as she worked to release a large black gelding. The horse was crazed with fear, its eyes rolling and its front hooves pounding the dirt.

She was still pulling the stall board out of the way when the horse bolted. Its shoulder knocked into the wood with enough force to knock her backwards. She landed hard on her rump.

She broke into another fit of coughing, using her wrist and

forearm to try and block the smoke that only seemed heavier. There were two horses left.

When her coughs had subsided, she looked up to see a hand outstretched.

But it wasn't Nathan.

It was Rob, and his face was a thundercloud.

"I don't suppose you'd leave if I demanded it," he said as she allowed him to assist her to her feet.

She shook her head.

They separated and released the last two horses just as an ominous creak from overhead sounded. The building shifted, and a curtain of sparks flew down in a wicked spiral. Her heart crashed against her ribs.

"Let's go." He took her arm in his big hand, but she'd seen the two saddles—hers and Janie's—resting on an empty stall partition. She wrenched out of his grip and raced forward to grab one of them. Each saddle meant weeks of work, and if she could save one...

She heard an audible sigh from the man behind her, but as she turned with the heavy saddle in her arms, he was there to pick up the second one.

They raced for the door even as another shower of sparks descended.

As they passed into the fresh air, the building gave another groan, and the ceiling caved in, dropping fire, boards, and sparks all around.

Liza stumbled toward the house, her lungs and throat burning, her eyes watering. She dropped the saddle halfway across the yard. Rob did the same, turning on her and clutching her shoulders.

"That was incredibly stupid," he boomed. His eyes were as wild as the horse that'd knocked her down.

She shook off his hold and took a step back. Her own terror

manifested in sharp words. "The saddles were *right there*. And we were leaving the building anyway. They take weeks to create. And I can't afford to lose them."

Her tirade over, she dissolved into another bout of coughing.

Rob was staring at her, his eyes unfathomable, still breathing with difficulty, as affected by the smoke as she had been.

"Rob!" Nathan called, and the moment was broken as the rancher joined his friend to carry buckets from the trough—where Mindy still pumped, bless her—to the burning barn. The horses ran free in the field behind, tossing their heads and prancing nervously.

She'd join the men in a moment, but for now stood with her hands propped on her knees, trying to catch her breath.

She studied the structure and knew theirs was a losing endeavor. Fire licked up one entire wall of the barn, and the ceiling had already collapsed.

Poor Nathan.

IT WOULD BE a long time before Rob forgot Liza's soot-smudged face and the fierceness in her voice when she'd berated him.

Nathan's barn was a total loss. The nearest neighbors had arrived just after the roof had collapsed and the sky dumped its load of rain.

He'd stood beside Nathan and watched the structure fall. With the rains, the grass had been wet enough to keep the fire from spreading to the house and the fields. But Nathan's devastation had been plain to see. Losing the season's hay and the structure itself was a huge setback.

Rob had planned to return home after delivering the two

Bennett sisters back to Calvin, but now his plans were on hold. He wouldn't leave Nathan in such a pickle. He was a better friend than that. Besides, his ranch foreman had things well under control.

Rob and another neighbor had made quick repair to the corral, and now Rob rode out in the falling dark to round up the horses he and Liza—mostly Liza—had set loose.

The first two had come easily at his whistle, but the four remaining animals were skittish after the fire earlier, and that required he give chase. They couldn't run forever.

Unfortunately, the task gave him too much time to think about Liza Bennett.

From that first night when he'd learned she was Maude's daughter, he'd judged her.

But the Liza he'd come to know on Nate's ranch was a surprise. She'd been a fierce protector for her sister and had stubbornly doctored Janie all night long. She'd pitched in immediately to help with breakfast chores, not allowing herself to be treated as a guest in Nate's home.

And then this afternoon, she'd wrangled Mindy to help put the fire out when they'd needed it most, not giving the other girl a chance to refuse.

Finally, she'd run into the burning barn, put herself in danger, to save the horses. She could have just saved her father's two, but she'd stayed, freed them all.

And the vulnerability in her expression when she'd revealed that her family couldn't afford to lose two saddles...

He was quite sure she hadn't meant for him to see that.

Now that he knew, he couldn't forget.

Liza was real. She was something special.

And he'd been making missteps since the first moment they'd met.

9

The second morning after the fire, Janie worked at hanging clean laundry on the line outside Nathan's house. Across the yard, the remains of the barn—one wall remained standing above the rubble—were charred and dark.

With the second round of storms, the creek had continued to flood its banks. And the two men had been working nonstop all day yesterday, with no time to deliver the women to town, even if the creek had subsided.

There was no way Janie was getting on a horse by herself anytime soon.

One pair of men's pants, the soot washed away under Liza's hands inside. One man's shirt. Bedsheets that still smelled slightly of smoke.

The simple task made her shoulder ache and stole her breath. She bent in half, pressing her hand against her burning chest. With the sheets blocking anyone from seeing her from the house, Janie could catch her breath and finish hanging the laundry to dry without her sister insisting she rest. Her chest still hurt, but not like it had that first night. Her persistent cough remained, but she was hopeful it, too, would pass in a few days.

Hoofbeats approached, and Janie straightened, but her chest tightened as she tried to steady her breathing.

Nathan. He was already off the horse. "Are you well?"

"Yes." She stiffened her spine. "Of course."

He glanced to the house. "Your warden allowed you out of the house?"

She couldn't help smiling at that. "She's been particularly strict, but I finally wore her down."

"And your shoulder?"

"I'll survive," she said dryly. It ached with activity and when she rolled onto it in her sleep.

"I'm glad to see your health is improving. I'm sorry that I haven't been such a good host." He stopped several feet away, and she could see the streak of soot across his jaw. He and Rob had spent all day yesterday attempting to salvage what could be saved from the wreckage of the barn and clearing the burned wood. They'd missed lunch completely and come in for a late supper drooping with exhaustion, smelling of sweat and smoke.

"You've done more than enough. I'm sorry we've inconvenienced you just as you're setting up house."

His eyes were warm, and her stomach swooped in response to his look. Maybe, if they could forget the impropriety of her rescue, there could be hope for...

His gaze slid past her, and his brow wrinkled. She turned to follow his gaze and saw a wagon trundling toward the farmhouse, still at least a half mile away.

She would recognize the three bonnets with their gaudy plumes anywhere. Mama and her younger sisters.

Her time with Nathan was up.

Heart pounding, she turned back to Nathan, spoke quickly.

"I wanted to ask you… it's important to me that my mother not find out about… about what happened between us the night you rescued me."

"What do you mean? Rob already told his sister, the marshal, about the rescue. It's probably all around town that you recovered here." Some of the warmth had disappeared from his eyes.

"Not that part."

He extended one hand toward her. "I don't understand."

"When you rescued me, my skirt... I wasn't… I wasn't clothed properly." She was making a mess of this. Partly because she could hear echoes of Albert's mother Edna screaming at her in her memories. *Brazen hussy! Filthy seductress!*

Tears rose in her throat, but she ruthlessly quashed them.

"It wasn't like that," he said quietly, all emotion now stripped from his face. All the warmth gone.

She swallowed hard.

"Nothing untoward happened," he said.

"Exactly." The wagon was so close now that she could hear the plod of the horses' hooves, the creak of their harness. "So there's no reason Mama needs to know every single detail."

She could see from the lines in Nathan's brow that he didn't understand. He couldn't know. And she wouldn't tell him. She would never, *ever* speak of Albert.

His mouth opened as if he would question her further.

But the farmhouse door opened and closed. "Janie!" Liza called.

And there was Rob, walking over from the barn.

Mindy was nowhere to be seen.

There was no more time for her awkward explanations as Mama's wagon entered the yard.

Janie left the rest of the laundry in its basket and met Liza at the bottom porch step, Nathan following. Liza put her arm around Janie's waist, and she was grateful for the contact, the support.

Mama reined in the two horses. Not very well, and Rob jogged the last two steps to catch their bridles and draw them to a stop.

"Oh, Janie!" Mama's dramatic wail sent instant heat into her face. Must Mama always be this way?

Nathan glanced at Janie briefly, and her face burned hotter. She'd just effectively confessed to him that Mama wasn't to be trusted.

Mama accepted Rob's help over the wagon wheel and rushed forward to throw her arms around Janie, dislodging her from Liza's hold. She gave a convincing little sob, though when she moved back to peer into Janie's face, her eyes were dry.

Janie held in a wince.

Liza had no compunction about setting Mama straight. "She'll be all right, Mama. Doc can check on her cough once we're back home, but she's in one piece, thanks to Mr. Bingley."

"And Mr. Darcy," Janie added.

Rob's expression was unreadable as he stared at Liza.

Kitty and Lydia had been helped from the wagon and stared wide-eyed at the burned-out shell of the barn.

"Oh, yes," Mama gushed, turning to the men. "Thank you ever so much, Mr. Bingley."

Nathan took off his hat and swept one hand over his head. Beneath the hat, sweat had matted and curled his hair, and he had the grace to look embarrassed more than anything else. "I only wish I could've done more. Acted more quickly."

Mama sent a calculating look between Nathan and Janie.

But it was Lydia who spoke. "Mr. Bingley, your barn..."

Nathan sighed, mashing his hat back on his head. "Yes,

we've had an unfortunate lightning strike. Although we can be glad it didn't hit the house." His smile was a little stiff.

Rob leveled a look on Lydia, then Mama. "Don't you mean 'the Parrott's barn?' Or the barn that belongs to the town?"

Mama colored a little but raised her chin a notch. "Word in town is that Mr. Bingley has already purchased the place."

Janie had no doubt as to who had ferreted out that information.

"Seems kind of dishonest to let rumors float about that one's just *looking* at a ranch." Mama let the shrewd statement hang suggestively.

Rob sighed softly. Mama didn't hear or ignored it.

Kitty seemed oblivious as she blurted, "You should have a barn raising, Mr. Bingley!"

Lydia was quick to grab on to the idea. "Oh, that would be delightful! You could invite everyone in town and all your neighbors and there could be dancing and—"

"Lydia," Liza interrupted softly.

Rob grimaced, quickly stifled, but Nathan seemed to like the idea. His face had lit up. "I think we just might."

10

"Papa, this line doesn't total—" Liza's words cut off as she pushed through the curtain separating the storeroom from the store proper.

Papa was waiting on a customer, a pair of black dress boots between them on the counter, and Liza pulled back slightly.

When the customer had finished her transaction and left with the boots boxed up, Liza moved through the curtain and into the shop.

Papa put a pair of brown dress boots behind the counter. "You've been going through the account books again, haven't you?"

She put the heavy, leather-bound ledger on the counter and opened it to the page she'd marked with a ribbon. She ran her finger down one of the columns. "Look here. I've spent an hour on this column, and it doesn't total."

Papa rested his hand atop hers, flattening it on the book. "The books are not your concern. The store is not your concern. It's mine to worry over. Mine and your mother's."

Not true.

Not since Cottonwood Cove. Not since Liza had cost the family everything.

"Papa—"

"Liza," he countered with a twinkle in his eyes. "You're the smartest of your sisters. If by some chance, some man doesn't come to his senses and snatch you up and marry you, the store will be yours. But that won't happen until you're an old maid."

She pulled a face at him. She had no prospects. And didn't want any, not when she still owed so much to her family.

"You're young. Go upstairs and talk dresses with your sisters. They can't seem to talk of anything else."

Not since Nathan had invited the entire town to his barn raising this coming Saturday. Only Janie had been quiet, almost reticent about the event.

"Papa, I'd rather—"

"If you won't, then I'm going to go upstairs and have lunch." He grinned. "You'll mind the store?"

She sighed. "Of course."

Papa disappeared behind the curtain. She heard his tread on the stairs.

Moments later, Lydia and Kitty entered through the curtain, their chatter preceding them.

"I can't decide between the puffed sleeves or the capped." Lydia said with a toss of her hair. She and Kitty pored over a ladies' magazine held between them, Kitty pointing at one of the pages.

Had Papa needed some peace and quiet and sent them downstairs? It was tempting to send them right back up, but Liza refrained.

"Lydia," she said. "Could you please organize the window display?"

Lydia shook her head. "I don't want to. Why don't you do it?"

"Designing our new dresses for Mr. Bingley's barn raising is important, Liza," Kitty chimed in.

She ground her teeth. Keeping the family fed and a roof over their heads was important.

Unless Papa's store had an infusion of cash, imagining frocks that weren't likely to materialize was not.

But she didn't have the patience to convince her sisters to do the work today.

She abandoned the ledger, grateful for a temporary reprieve, even if she wouldn't admit it. The town of Calvin had supported their store well for the first two years after they'd moved here. These past three, sales of their leather goods had seen a steady decrease. If they suffered another bad year, they could lose everything.

She continued to ponder the problem as Lydia and Kitty chattered behind the counter. In the wide store window, morning sunlight fell warm across her face and arms. She eyed the painted wooden shelf Papa had always used to display goods that would catch the eyes of a passerby and the assortment of boots, wallets, a coin purse, and a saddlebag that were to be displayed on it.

The display needed something more... but what?

The jaunty bell over the door rang, interrupting her thoughts.

She was nearest the door and looked up... and up... into a pair of laughing hazel eyes.

"I saw your display, and I had to come in to inspect the wares more closely." The man's voice hinted at humor, and his smile had a slightly rakish cast to it.

Liza turned a circle, looking at the shelf and attempting to guess what he might've been looking at. "Oh, I'm not finished decorating. Did you want the saddlebag?"

A peal of giggles from behind the counter interrupted her.

The man shot a wink at her two sisters and then smiled down at her.

And Liza belatedly realized he'd been talking about her. *She* was the window display he'd wanted to get a closer look at.

How flirtatious.

And yet, his blatant admiration didn't bother her as it probably should have. She warmed from the inside and found a smile crossing her lips.

"Hello, Mr. Wickham!" Kitty called out.

"How are you today?" Lydia echoed.

He doffed his hat in her sisters' direction without breaking eye contact with Liza, and that set them off in another bout of giggles. She really should talk to Mama about their behavior.

"George Wickham, at your service," he said quietly.

"I'm Liza Bennett. My papa—"

"Owns this shop," he interrupted smoothly. "I had the pleasure of meeting your sisters just three days ago."

While she and Janie had been confined to Nathan's ranch.

"Lydia mentioned she had two older sisters, but she didn't confess how lovely you were."

Liza felt a blush rising. Janie was usually the recipient of such compliments, not her. She wasn't entirely sure how she should respond to it.

It certainly salved wounds still scabbed over from Rob Darcy's dismissal that first night.

She remembered the flash of his dark eyes in the smoke-filled barn.

And then, as if she'd conjured him with her thoughts, Rob was there, passing before her window.

From the boardwalk, he tipped his hat to her as Wickham stepped closer—into Rob's line of sight. Rob stopped mid-motion, a dark scowl crossing his features. He instantly turned on his heel and strode away.

What—?

A glance over her shoulder showed Lydia and Kitty whispering behind their hands at the counter. Had they seen Rob? She doubted it.

She turned back to Wickham, whose brows had knit together. His gaze remained on the window where Rob had disappeared.

"Do you know Mr. Darcy?" she asked.

Mr. Wickham came back to himself, smiling slightly at her.

Before he could say anything, three women pushed through the door, chatting and instantly casting curious looks at Liza and her companion.

He doffed his hat and then looked back at Liza.

"If I might call on you tonight, perhaps we could talk more then?"

She couldn't help being flattered at his interest, especially after Rob Darcy's indifference. What could a simple walk around town hurt?

"He said he was close with Rob and Danna's grandfather before the man died."

Liza ran her hairbrush through locks that fell almost to her waist. She and Janie shared a bed in the room that faced Main Street in the family's quarters above their shop. The room was small, and a second bed, one that Lydia and Kitty shared, was crowded against the opposite wall, leaving the girls little space to maneuver.

And even less for private conversations.

Janie sat huddled with her knees up beneath her blanket, braiding her hair down her back. The doctor had agreed that her lingering cough wasn't life-threatening and she should resume regular activities unless she felt fatigued.

She'd spent hours in the minuscule reading nook, which they'd built beside the window above Main Street, since they'd returned from the Bingleys' ranch. Liza didn't know what to make of it. She'd thought Janie and Nathan made a good match, had thought Nathan was sweet on Janie. But Janie seemed more withdrawn than happy.

Lydia and Kitty whispered and giggled from their bed, but that didn't mean they weren't listening. They'd certainly been interested in Mr. Wickham when he'd visited the shop earlier, asking Liza what he'd had to say and watching out the window when he'd called for her to take a turn about town on his arm.

Liza remembered the conversation they'd had on their way. "He was supposed to have received an inheritance, but Rob cheated him out of it."

"What?" Janie shook her head. "Rob doesn't seem like the kind of man who'd do something like that."

Liza had to smile at Janie's quick defense. "You never like to see the bad in anyone, Janie-girl."

Janie wrinkled her nose. "I don't think Nathan would be friends with someone who would be so unkind, do you?"

That was more like the Janie Liza knew. The one who would filter her perception of Rob Darcy's character through the man who'd rescued her.

"You didn't see the way Rob looked at him," Liza murmured. She shivered just thinking about the black look Rob had delivered the other man. "There was definitely bad blood between them."

And didn't she know how difficult Rob could be? He'd been highhanded and bossy during Janie's ordeal and plenty stern when he hadn't agreed with her about the saddles during the fire.

"Hmm."

Janie's noncommittal hum did nothing but spark her

temper. She strove to push it down. She'd been attracted to Rob initially, and he'd insulted her. But she wasn't one to think the worst of someone just because he didn't like her. Was she?

She didn't know George Wickham either, but he'd charmed her with his compliments—less effusive and more believable in private—and stories of his mother and sister back home in St. Louis.

"The Bingleys' barn raising is Saturday. Should I ask Nathan about it?"

"No." Liza raised her chin. "If Rob has a defense against the accusations, he can tell me directly."

Which she couldn't imagine happening. Rob didn't care one whit what she thought. No doubt he'd soon be returning to his own ranch, and they'd never see each other again. That was fine with her. She was plenty busy with the store.

And George... he'd taken a job on a nearby spread. Perhaps they could get to know each other better.

"Girls!" Mama burst into the room, startling Liza into dropping her brush on the wood floor. She bent to pick it up.

"Your father just shared some exciting news," Mama bubbled.

Liza stifled a groan as she straightened. She and Janie shared a glance. *Everything* got Mama excited.

"Do you remember Mr. Collins? He's your father's second cousin, once removed. Or... I can't remember, exactly. A very distant relation."

Kitty and Lydia sat up in bed, attentive to Mama's every word.

"Apparently, he's the proprietor of a very successful store in Sheridan, and he's coming to visit Papa and the store."

Liza's stomach churned. "What is the purpose of his visit?" Was he here to convince Papa to sell the store? She'd seen a notation in one of Papa's ledgers about an offer to purchase the store, something she hadn't heard Papa or Mama mention before.

"Something about the store, but really, Liza, the more important thing is that I believe he is *single*."

Mama's eyes were shining in her excitement, but all Liza could think about was the store. If he was here to buy it, where did that leave their family? They'd had to leave everything behind once before—Liza's fault. Could the family bear it again?

Mama seemed to be waiting for some response, her avid gaze fixed on Liza.

"I'm certain we will all be glad to get to know a distant relation." She was careful to encompass all three of her sisters with the sweep of her arm.

"I'm certain Liza hopes he isn't ugly," Lydia said before hiding wild giggles in her pillow.

Mama propped her fists on her hips. "Really, Liza. You aren't getting any younger, you know. And you've turned away every eligible man in Calvin."

"And most of the neighboring ranches," Kitty pointed out.

Liza bit her tongue to keep from directing Mama's criticism toward Janie. She well knew how sensitive Janie was—all of them did—and so she allowed herself to be the one Mama harangued about the necessity of getting married.

Since Nathan's daring rescue, Mama seemed to be fixed on a match between Mr. Bingley and Janie.

"I see no rush to get married," Liza said. "While Papa needs my help at the store."

"Pish," Mama said. "Your father has me and the younger girls to help him keep shop."

Yes, but Mama was too often flitting around town on social calls to be of much help in the store, and Lydia and Kitty were no help at all.

Mama leveled a finger toward Liza. "I want you to think about catching Mr. Collins's fancy."

She left the room in a swirl of her nightrail, and Lydia and Kitty subsided into more giggles and whispers as Janie doused the lamp.

But when Liza stared into the darkness as the other girls fell off to sleep, it wasn't the unknown Mr. Collins or even Mr. Wickham's smiling eyes that kept her awake.

It was Rob and the look of utter contempt she'd last seen on his face.

11

Mr. Collins was not single, much to Mama's chagrin.

His wife, Charlotte, was petite with blond hair. And very pregnant.

"Don't worry so much," Charlotte Collins whispered to Liza from the back of the shop.

Right now, her husband stood with Papa, pointing at the window display that Liza had spent hours meticulously arranging. He was frowning and shaking his head.

Liza felt sick. Was it that bad?

"William is very good at managing his Sheridan store," Charlotte said.

Liza shifted her attention to the customer who stood nearby, fiddling with an arrangement of belt buckles atop the counter.

Liza tried to find a smile, but it was difficult. "I'm sure he is. But this is Calvin, not Sheridan. And this is our store."

Charlotte's eyes twinkled. "It certainly isn't Sheridan. Our accommodations at the boardinghouse are—never mind that." She stopped the complaint before she finished.

"Does your William intend to buy Papa's store?" Liza asked.

No matter how slyly she'd asked, she hadn't been able to get a straight answer from Papa since Mama had announced Mr. Collins's visit.

Charlotte shrugged. "He hasn't said. He's invested in two other stores—one in Idaho and one in Denver, Colorado, and has made quite a pretty profit." She smiled sweetly. "But that doesn't mean your store would be a good investment for him."

Lydia and Kitty stormed into the storeroom, arguing animatedly about a pair of gloves.

"Girls!"

Kitty gave a convincing pout. "You always shush us."

Lydia was quick to join in. "You used to play games with us, help us with our hair ribbons, and now all you think about is Papa's shop!"

Heat filled Liza's face. She felt the weight of Charlotte's curious stare.

"Can we talk about this later?" she asked.

Lydia huffed and shrugged, but then she saw a friend passing on the boardwalk outside the store. Both girls rushed out to say hello.

"Please excuse my sisters," Liza said to Charlotte, who watched them with an amused expression. "They are single-minded in their pursuit of matrimony." Same as Mama. "If we could harness only a fraction of their energy toward making the store a success..."

Charlotte smiled, one hand rubbing the bump of her belly. She shrugged. "Perhaps the problem isn't the store at all. Perhaps the town is too small to sustain it."

The thought sent turmoil roiling through Liza. It must've shown on her face, because Charlotte hurried on. "Or perhaps that's not it at all. If William can help your papa, he will."

Mama demanded they break for lunch upstairs, and Charlotte was quickly distracted by the mention of food.

Liza was not so easily deterred. She sat on the stairs as Mama and Papa disappeared with the Collinses.

Was Charlotte right? Was the town of Calvin too small to support their family's business?

How could that be, when father had made a good profit in the beginning? Had the demand for leather goods really diminished that much in such a short period of time?

Should they just give up?

She couldn't think that. She'd set her mind to fixing everything she'd ruined when they'd had to leave Cottonwood Cove. She couldn't give up now.

Lydia's complaint popped to the forefront of her thoughts. It was true Kitty and Lydia's preoccupation with fashion and friends and men annoyed her. It was also true that she spent most of her time devising ways to help the store.

But she hadn't known her sisters wished for her company, her opinions.

NATE SPIED Janie across Calvin's dusty Main Street and found himself crossing the lane before he'd even realized he intended to. He hadn't seen her in ten days, not since she'd urged him to speak carefully around her mother.

He hadn't known what to make of that. Was she embarrassed because of the situation they'd found themselves in? Surely that must have been it.

That uncertainty about Janie and the ranch had kept him from town. He and Rob had cleared away the rubble of the burned-out barn, cut and hauled new beams, and ordered supplies for the barn raising tomorrow. Everything was ready.

Would Janie be there?

Right now, she wore a simple navy dress and jaunty bonnet of the same color that made her blond hair stand out.

She was talking with another young woman outside the milliner's shop, and both ladies turned to him with surprise as his boots hit the boardwalk on their side of the street.

"Miss Bennett." He tipped his hat, unable to keep from smiling at the flash of her blue eyes.

"Nath—I mean, Mr. Bingley." She stumbled over the greeting, and her friend noticed, staring between them with a curious gaze.

Janie's cheeks pinked. "Mr. Bingley, may I present my friend Merritt Harding?"

He tipped his hat. "Hello." To Janie, "Are you on your way home? May I walk with you?"

"I won't keep you, Janie dear," the woman said. "We'll catch up soon." She departed with an arch look that he couldn't interpret.

And then he was alone with Janie. Sort of alone, as they were in plain sight on the boardwalk.

He fell into step beside her, jutting out his elbow so she might hold onto him. But her hands stayed folded over a small brown-wrapped package held against her midsection. Her bonnet hid her eyes, and he couldn't tell whether she'd seen his gesture or not. Was she shy, or did she simply not want to hold onto him?

His thoughts flashed to Hildy and the disdainful look she'd worn as she'd looked at him that last time.

He straightened his shoulders against the pain of it and cast about for a neutral topic.

She coughed once into her gloved hand, the sound a reminder of what she'd suffered that one terrible night.

"How is your health?" he asked.

"I am much improved." The pink in her cheeks seemed to prove the statement.

"I'm glad." He couldn't keep the warmth from his voice, and she glanced at him, her bonnet tilting to give him a glimpse of her eyes.

"How is your sister?" she asked.

"She is... much the same." His disappointment was keen, and she must've heard it in his voice because her face turned toward him again, her eyes warm and curious.

"I wanted... I had hoped for a close relationship," he explained. "But it seems hopeless now." They were too different, he and Mindy. She hadn't come out and said that she judged him for being his father's illegitimate offspring, but perhaps that's where part of her animosity stemmed from. "I suppose it shouldn't matter. I've been on my own for a long time."

"What do you mean?"

"I suppose Liza told you about—about my parentage." He stumbled over the word as hot shame, old as it was, rose up to choke him.

They approached a broken step where the boardwalk dropped them into a side street, and he reached out to support her elbow as they crossed it. For a moment, she was turned toward him, and he glimpsed such warmth in her eyes that a responding emotion rose in his chest, quick and sure.

A horse blew from nearby, clopping hoofbeats approaching, and he ushered her across the side street to the next patch of boardwalk.

"Liza only mentioned that you'd lost your parents."

Bless her. He hadn't expected that, had thought surely Liza would tell Janie his family legacy that had spilled on the dining table like so much horse manure.

And now he wondered if he could back away from this

conversation he'd introduced. Janie didn't know that he was the product of an affair, didn't know about his mother or the childhood that had been so difficult.

Would she look at him differently, if she knew?

Rob would know how to get out of this situation, to tell her part of it without revealing the entirety of his shame. But he wasn't Rob.

He was only Nathan. A man who couldn't spin a lie to save his life.

They were approaching her family's store, but she slowed her steps.

And he remembered Hildy's disdain, but what could he do?

He ducked his head, letting his Stetson shade his eyes and maybe hide part of the shame. "My mother met my father when she was seventeen. He charmed her and he—and they..." He couldn't say the words, hoped she understood. "He was already married."

She inhaled softly. Surprised.

"When I was conceived, he sent my mother West, and we never heard from him again. My mother worked her fingers to the bone to put food on the table and clothes on our backs."

She drew him to a stop with a gentle hand on his arm.

She'd reached for him!

She looked up at him. In her expressive eyes, he saw... compassion.

"You must've loved her very much."

He nodded, words clogging in his throat in a hot knot. He cleared it away. "She died when I was sixteen, and I've been cowboying ever since. Then Mindy arrived at Rob's ranch with news of an inheritance and," he exhaled noisily, laughing a little at the disbelief he still felt, "I didn't even know I had a half-sister."

Someone passed on the boardwalk, and Janie took a self-conscious step back, her hand falling away. She turned her head, her bonnet hiding her eyes from him again.

But he wouldn't soon forget the way she'd looked at him. Touched him.

"Mindy's father—my father—left her a goodly part of the inheritance, but she won't receive it until her twenty-first birthday. She's angry with him... and with me. She finds life here difficult and boring."

He wanted to ask whether Janie thought she'd find life on the ranch difficult. But that was certainly a presumptuous question. He liked her. But did she return his affection?

"Maybe..." Janie started. She considered the issue, and a few too many heartbeats passed while he waited to hear what she would say. "Maybe I could speak with her tomorrow. At the barn raising."

She lifted her eyes to him, and he couldn't help the warm smile that suffused his face. "That would be... I would welcome it."

She nodded, shyly turning away again.

He walked with her the final few steps to her family's store, and she went inside with a demure "goodbye."

He hadn't intended to seek Janie out in town—their meeting had been serendipitous. And he left with his spirits lightened, not even thinking about the work ahead.

12

The morning of the barn raising dawned clear and mild, the perfect weather for a workday.

Riding in the wagon, Liza couldn't help but notice that Janie was a bundle of nerves. She'd been fidgety and even cross with Lydia as they'd readied to leave town this morning, a rarity for her usually even-tempered sister.

Mr. Collins and his Charlotte had begged to come along for the event, eager to attend for reasons Liza couldn't fathom. Riding in a wagon for an hour and a half couldn't be comfortable for someone in Charlotte's condition, though the journey was almost over now.

With Charlotte beside her and Lydia and Kitty giggling across the wagon, she couldn't find out what was bothering Janie.

Mr. Collins rode on horseback beside the wagon, talking with Papa.

"I've never been to a barn raising before," Charlotte said. She swept one hand across her cheek, catching several strands of hair that had escaped her bun. "How many people will be there?"

Judging from the line of wagons throwing up dust before and after the Bennetts' wagon, it would be a good turnout.

"Most of the town. The men will do most of the work," Liza said. "We'll have plenty of time to visit. Then we'll spend the afternoon preparing a big meal. If there's enough progress made and if the mayor brought his banjo, we might even get to enjoy some dancing before the evening is over."

Charlotte's eyes danced. "I love dancing, although I don't move as quickly as I used to." She inclined her head to include Janie in the conversation. "Will you introduce me to your beau?"

Janie colored. "I don't have a beau," she mumbled, ducking her head to play with one of the pleats of her skirt.

"Oh. Your mother said there was a Mr...."

Mama turned in the wagon's bench seat, almost toppling Papa. "Don't be ridiculous, Janie, dear. I told Charlotte all about Mr. Bingley."

Charlotte's expression lit. "Yes, that's it!"

Janie looked back at Mama. "Mr. Bingley is only a friend."

Mama smirked. "Pish posh. You spent several days on his ranch."

Color leached from Janie's face.

"Janie *recuperated* there, thanks to Mr. Bingley's generosity," Liza interjected. "And it wasn't as if we had a choice, as the storms had flooded the creek."

Charlotte's expression was slightly chagrined, as if she were sorry she'd brought it up at all.

"Nothing *happened*," Janie said, and her voice was tighter than Liza had ever heard it.

Mama shrugged. "It doesn't mean the man can't be *encouraged* to make something happen. In fact, I'll take it upon myself to make sure Mr. Bingley pays attention to you today."

"Mama," Liza protested.

Mama smiled, smug that her idea was just right.

"I would prefer you didn't," Janie said. Her eyes sparkled, a little wild, and Liza thought perhaps unshed tears gave them their sheen.

But Mama just shrugged and turned back toward the front.

Janie frowned.

Liza tried to catch her eye, to give her an assurance that she would help corral Mama, keep him from Nathan today. Janie had confessed that Nathan had approached her in town and walked her home. The hope shining in Janie's face had excited Liza. Janie *liked* Nathan, even if she wouldn't say it outright. All the more reason for Liza to keep Mama out of the way to let the relationship progress.

The wagon creaked up to the Bingleys' ranch, and Papa pulled to a stop in a line of other wagons. Men and women were already gathering for the event, and children ran, laughing and shouting.

After settling the horses, Papa and Mr. Collins joined the men at the worksite next to the old burned-out barn. One side of the new barn had already been framed and raised toward the sky.

Lydia and Kitty rushed off to speak to their friends, and Mama made introductions for Charlotte nearby. Janie unloaded a picnic blanket.

Liza stood in the wagon bed and shaded her eyes as she searched among the men for the one person she wanted to see. Mr. Wickham. She had seen him one other time in town, when he'd been charming and suave. He'd promised to attend today's event.

But she didn't see him anywhere. And instead, her eyes found Rob Darcy at the corner of the new structure. His broad-shouldered figure was instantly recognizable as he held a tall post upright. Her chest banded tight.

And then he turned his head and his gaze landed on her. She felt it like a touch and quickly knelt in the wagon. It was too bad he hadn't returned to his own ranch and left her in peace. The man irritated her like a boot that didn't fit. And left blisters.

"Can you hand me the basket?" Janie pointed to the overloaded picnic basket at the rear of the wagon.

Liza's back was turned while she reached for it.

"Hallo."

Liza glanced over her shoulder to see Nathan had approached.

"Hello," Janie said quietly. She turned slightly away from him.

Nathan's welcoming smile faded.

Liza craned her neck to see where Mama had gone—there, two wagons over, talking to Mrs. Kimball.

"Are you well, Liza?"

She sent the man a smile. "Yes. And you? It's a lovely morning to build a new barn."

Nathan shifted on his feet. He took off his hat, put it back on. "You'll both save me a dance tonight, won't you?"

"Of course."

"I don't know."

Liza's instant acceptance nearly drowned out Janie's soft near-refusal. Janie glanced toward Mama quickly.

Had she even seen Nathan's disappointed expression?

"We partnered well at the town dance, didn't we?" he asked.

Janie nodded slightly.

Mama left off her conversation and started their way, dragging Charlotte.

"I suppose I should go find Mindy," Janie said quickly. "I haven't forgotten my promise. Will you excuse me?"

Nathan stood looking after her as she strode toward the ranch house.

Liza sat on the end of the wagon and slipped to the ground. Why was Janie acting so strangely? Was Mama's inference in the wagon that she would say something to Nathan causing Janie to act like this? Or was it something more?

"I'd better get to work." He doffed his hat to Liza, making a convenient escape just before Mama arrived.

Liza remained unsure about Janie's brisk departure. If she was unsure, the man must be even more so.

JANIE FOUND Mindy hiding in the farmhouse kitchen peering through the window. When Janie entered with a soft knock, she jumped back, a guilty expression crossing her features.

After Mama's antics in the wagon, Janie wanted to hide away, too. Nathan had come to say hello, and Janie had panicked. When he'd asked her to dance, she'd been afraid that Mama would see them together and start spreading rumors.

What a disaster.

"You should come out and join us," Janie said, offering the girl a warm smile. She well knew how scary new faces could be. "I'm happy to introduce you to the other girls from town. We're a nice bunch."

"I'd rather not," Mindy said stiffly.

Oh. "My sisters are out there," she tried again. "You didn't get to meet them when they came out to fetch Liza and me."

"No thank you." Mindy pointed her nose toward the ceiling.

Why must the girl be such a pill? Janie reminded herself that Mindy'd lost her parents and probably felt adrift.

There was a pause as Janie tried to think of a way to persuade the girl to come out.

"Nathan would appreciate it if you made an effort," she said finally.

"I'm sure he would. But I won't be in Calvin long enough for it to matter."

What did that mean?

"Never mind." Mindy flounced toward the parlor. "Why don't you go back outside and join the rest of the girls angling to marry my brother."

Heat suffused Janie's face. "I'm not—"

"There's no use pretending. I see the way you look at him. And I'm not going out."

Mindy whirled and rushed up the stairs. Moments later, a door slammed.

What had Mindy meant by her statement, *I won't be in Calvin long enough for it to matter*?

She remembered Nathan's expression on the boardwalk. *She finds life here difficult and boring.* It was clear he wanted a relationship with Mindy, but she wasn't willing to budge.

Had Mindy said what she'd said about Janie out of spite?

Between Mama's finagling and Mindy's accusation about her motives, all the anticipation Janie had had for this event had turned to dread.

Rob couldn't help being aware of Liza throughout the morning.

While he and an entire crew of townsmen constructed the four walls of the barn, she circled among the women with her arm threaded through her mother's, chatting and talking. They passed close to the barn site once, but not close enough for him to make out their conversation.

He couldn't stop thinking about seeing her with Wickham

in the store. The memory stole his sleep. And was the first thing he'd thought about this morning.

He should warn her about the man's likely wicked intentions. Wickham. Wicked.

But warning her hadn't been the first thought on his mind when he'd seen them together.

A stab of what could only be described as jealousy had pierced him. He'd wanted to walk into the store and bodily remove her from Wickham's presence.

He'd left instead.

Possibly, the man had only been in the store to make a purchase.

But Rob had reacted to Liza's warm smile.

Had she ever smiled at *him* quite like that?

As the day wore on, the weather warmed considerably, and at one point, the crew he was working with took a break. He stood in the shade of the house and gulped cool water from the pail being passed around. He couldn't help dumping a dipper-full over his head, relishing the feel of cool streams flowing down his neck. He pulled at the front of his shirt, releasing it where it stuck to his skin.

And he noticed Liza across the way, staring. She held a baby on her hip, and a little girl tugged on her skirt.

When their gazes collided, she flushed and turned away.

She wasn't unaffected by him.

But was she involved with Wickham?

He was determined to find out.

He was on the framed roof when he heard her pealing laugh and nearly smashed his thumb with his hammer.

A glance to the ground revealed Liza with her mother and Janie, all three in conversation with Nathan, who was drinking from the dipper.

Janie's gaze flickered to Nathan and then away. Nathan

spoke animatedly, but Rob thought he read tension in the set of his friend's shoulders.

Mrs. Bennett laughed, but the sound rang false and made Rob grit his teeth.

Seeing them together reminded him that he hadn't come to Calvin seeking a wife for himself. He'd come to help Nathan get on his feet on the ranch. After what'd happened with Hildy, he'd also vowed to keep his friend from being hurt again.

Nathan spoke to Janie, and her eyes skittered away. She couldn't even look at him, wasn't smiling. Was she indifferent to him?

Rob wouldn't let his friend get hurt again. Even if he had to step in and say something about Janie Bennett.

"Liza?"

Evening shadows were falling as she turned, sure her eyes were wide at the query from Rob Darcy. He was close, between their wagon and the neighboring one. The family was assembled to eat their picnic supper, and no one seemed to have noticed his approach.

"Will you save a dance for me?" he asked.

The barn had taken shape over the course of the day. Now the sun was going down and the last of the wooden shingles were being applied to the roof. There was still work to be done on the barn's interior, but with the help of almost all of Calvin, Nathan had recovered much of what was lost.

And Rob wanted her to save him a dance?

The moment stretched long as his gaze and hers melded. She nodded, and he turned and strode away.

She squatted in the shadow of the wagon, heart pounding against her ribcage.

Had that just happened?

And why had she agreed?

She didn't even like Rob. He was highhanded and disdainful...

And he'd helped rescue Janie.

But he'd also mistreated George.

Her thoughts were a muddle.

Even before folks were finished eating, lanterns were lit inside the new barn. The empty building was perfect for dancing and visiting. The sound of a fiddle beckoned everyone inside.

Nathan approached their picnic blanket, his hand extended to Janie. She hesitated, and his smile fell.

"Oh, go on, Janie!" Mama encouraged.

Was Liza mistaken, or did she see a minuscule wince cross Janie's face at Mama's words? But Janie smiled tentatively, and Nathan's joy returned as she placed her hand in his. They were among the first inside, and Liza caught glimpses of her sister through the large open barn doors as Janie twirled in the dance.

Janie deserved a happily ever after. *Please, God.*

Kitty and Lydia disappeared into the new barn, as did Mr. and Mrs. Collins and Mama. Liza lingered on the picnic blanket gathering up plates and utensils. Long enough for Papa to ask, "Aren't you going to dance?"

And then Rob was there, appearing out of the shadows, hatless, his hair almost as dark as the night.

Heart racing, she stood.

He didn't offer his arm or take her hand as they approached the barn, where sounds of music and laughter filtered out. If she'd expected it, she would've been disappointed.

She didn't know what to expect from the enigmatic man.

Inside, the musicians called for everyone to square up. The

bow was drawn across the fiddle, and the caller gave their first set of directions.

Rob's hand closed over hers as he twirled her. His warm skin against hers ignited a cavalcade of sparks along her nerve endings.

If she'd been dancing with anyone else, she'd have welcomed it.

Unlike the other dancers, who smiled and laughed with each other, Rob's face was almost comically serious.

And she was filled with a sudden desire to draw some reaction out of him. Any reaction.

"I'm glad Nathan recovered his barn," she said as she passed by his shoulder, following the caller's directions. Her skirts swished against his pants. "It was a fine turnout."

"He must still bear the cost of the lost hay and farm implements."

She ground her teeth. Couldn't the man see anything positive?

"You seemed to enjoy yourself today," he said.

"You were watching?"

He whirled away from her, they crossed behind another pair of dancers. When they came together again, his jaw was clamped shut, and a muscle in his cheek ticked.

She bared her teeth in a fierce smile. "It isn't a crime to enjoy oneself. I don't often have a chance to visit friends who live out of town. Papa's shop keeps me too busy to make calls very often."

The caller demanded a different move, and Rob's hand settled at her waist, the weight of it hot and heavy. She was close enough that she had to tilt her face up to see his.

That moment, the connection between them expanded and slowed. His dark eyes glittered down to her. He didn't smile, but even so, there was no denying that he was handsome. Striking.

"But not too busy to flirt with your customers?" he said. "Or perhaps just one customer in particular?"

He spun her away, making her slightly dizzy even as his words registered and her temper sparked.

"Do you mean Mr. Wickham?" she asked sweetly. "He was charming enough when he came into the shop."

He stepped into her space, the jolting movement out of place among the dancers who were still spinning and laughing. His face was serious, almost angry. He drew her away from the dancers into a shadowed corner of the barn, not allowing her space to retreat.

No one seemed to notice.

"I suppose Mr. Wickham is a charming sort of snake."

How dare he? "At least he has the decency to attempt charm."

He stopped advancing on her, taken aback as if she'd slapped him.

The music ended, and in the sudden quiet, each of his breaths was audible.

And then his expression went carefully blank. He nodded once. "Thank you for the dance. And the enlightenment."

And he was gone.

13

"I hate it here! I want to go back to St. Louis!"

Mindy's shout preceded the slam of the back door by seconds.

Rob attempted to ignore both as he shoved the post-diggers into the ground, still soft from last week's storms. With the barn completed, they'd needed to adjust the corral fence to accommodate the new placement. A new post laid on the ground next to where he worked.

The morning sun gave him a headache. Or possibly it was the sleepless night he'd passed.

Liza's words about his lack of charm had run through his brain like a steam locomotive with no brakes. She found Wickham charming. Not him.

He'd come to grips with his lack of social graces a long time ago. But the recent events made him realize what that lack would cost him.

And ranch tasks wouldn't wait. The corral and a few other chores needed to be completed. They were down to the last of it.

It was time for him to return home.

Nathan trudged toward him from the farmhouse. Except for Mindy, his friend had things on the ranch well under control. The livestock was thriving. The barn had been rebuilt.

There was nothing for Rob here. And his ranch needed tending.

He swiped the back of one hand over his sweaty forehead, dislodging his hat slightly. He judged the depth of his hole to be sufficient, and Nathan hefted the fence post to place it.

Nathan gave an apologetic glance. "I'm sorry about Mindy."

Rob exchanged his post-diggers for a shovel and began packing dirt beside the post as Nathan held it steady.

"It isn't an easy life for a woman," he said. "My sister—" He didn't have to finish the sentence. Nate knew his history. Rob's actions had resulted in Danna almost dying when she'd been sixteen.

"I've been thinking about sending her back. To St. Louis. If she attends that girl's school for another year or two, she might meet some eligible man. Or at least be a year or two closer to her own inheritance."

Nate's shoulders drooped. His friend wasn't one to give up. Rob knew how much he'd wanted to connect with Mindy, to be a real brother and sister.

How much this must be hurting him.

"Do you want me to stay on and watch the place until you return?" If Nate left today, that meant another week in Calvin. If Rob stayed away from town, he wouldn't have to see Liza with Wickham.

"No." Nate rubbed one hand on the back of his neck. His expression revealed uncertainty. Something else was bothering him. He whirled, facing Rob directly. "Do you think Janie Bennett fancies me?"

Rob tapped the post, ensuring it was stable. Finally he had no choice but to return Nathan's direct look. "I don't know."

"I know her mother is..." Nathan cast about for a polite way to say what Rob was thinking.

"Obnoxious?" Rob suggested. "The biggest gossip in town?"

Nathan gave him a hard look. "That wouldn't really matter. If we married, we'd live on the ranch—"

"It wouldn't matter, if Janie fancied you," Rob said.

Nathan looked as if Rob had gut-punched him. "You *don't* think she fancies me."

Rob scrubbed a hand over his mouth. Liza was right. He didn't have a gentle way with words.

Nathan looked away, squinting in the sunlight. "I thought we'd made a connection. I had hoped... but last night she was..."

"Distracted?" That was kinder than what he wanted to say.

Nate let his gaze roam to the mountains in the distance, which were just visible on the horizon.

Rob swallowed hard. "An event like her almost drowning can cause a sort of forced intimacy. You saw her in a situation where she was weak. You rescued her, and she was grateful. But does that mean...?"

Nate continued to stare at nothing.

"Maybe you're right," Nate said after a long time.

Of course he was.

But that didn't mean he wasn't disappointed, for his friend's sake.

A MONTH after the barn raising, Janie huddled alone in the bed she shared with Liza.

It was happening again.

You chased my son like a brazen hussy.

Seductress.

You have shamed us.

"Janie?"

Liza's quiet question shook Janie out of her reverie but didn't do anything to soothe her breaking heart.

Liza stood in the bedroom doorway, her shock apparent as she took in Janie's appearance. No doubt her hair had come out of its pins and her face was blotchy from the tears she'd already shed.

"What happened? Mama sent me up to check on you."

Janie shook her head, swiping at the tears she couldn't seem to stop.

Liza closed the bedroom door and sat on the end of the bed. "Is it Nathan? Is he hurt or—"

"He's gone," Janie whispered.

Liza's brows wrinkled. "What do you mean, *gone*?"

Janie tossed Nathan's letter to the end of the bed, where her sister picked it up.

The same young boy who'd brought her Mindy's supper invitation weeks ago had brought another missive. Thank goodness she'd excused herself upstairs to read it.

She closed her eyes and buried her face on her bent knees again.

She didn't need to read it to remember its contents. The words were emblazoned on her memory.

Miss Bennett,

After much soul-searching, I believe the two of us have different hopes for our future. With bitter emotion, I must tell you that I cannot call on you socially any longer.

I will be delivering my sister to St. Louis and will see her settled there. I can only hope my absence will allow for any emotions to run their course and that we may resume a simple friendship upon my return.

Nathan Bingley

Liza looked up from the note, her eyes sympathetic. "It says he's coming back."

He might be returning, but he didn't want her.

She'd been so careful to ensure no one heard of the inappropriateness of his rescue. Careful to stay out of Mama's way, so that Mama couldn't push him to make declarations he didn't really mean.

And it had all been for nothing.

He didn't want her.

She didn't want to be here when he returned. She couldn't bear to face him.

...the two of us have different hopes for our future.

Humiliation surged. Did he know how much she'd fancied him?

But obviously he didn't feel the same.

She must find a way to escape Calvin, at least for a short time. Maybe then she could face him.

The bed shifted, and Liza sat beside her and slid one arm around Janie's shoulders as she cried.

14

Mrs. Collins suffered difficult delivery. Stop. Send Liza to mind the store. Stop.

TWO LITTLE LINES IN A TELEGRAPH, and Papa had urged Liza to pack up and get on the next north-bound train.

She'd argued that she should stay. Janie was due home in a week from the extended visit she'd made to Aunt Myrtle in Omaha. Liza couldn't forget Janie's near-silent tears when she'd received Nathan's note. Liza couldn't understand what had happened.

She'd promised herself that she would help Janie find happiness. But all that had resulted in encouraging a relationship with Nathan was heartache. She was not the kind of sister she wanted to be.

William Collins's telegraph had arrived yesterday. Today Liza had ridden on the steam train for eight hours, and now she'd been delivered to the station.

Cottonwood Cove, where she'd grown up, was roughly the

size of Calvin. As a young girl, she'd been to Cheyenne once, and that had been in the company of her family.

The bustle of Sheridan's train station, even at the evening hour, transfixed her. She clutched her satchel against her midsection as she scanned the station platform for any familiar face.

She couldn't help remembering that Rob Darcy's ranch was located near Sheridan. How near, she didn't know. Surely, in a city like this, they would never cross paths.

The passengers who'd disembarked along with her had already dispersed.

No Mr. Collins.

And apparently, he hadn't sent anyone after her, either.

Papa had pressed several coins into her hand just before she'd left the Calvin station. She'd hidden in the washroom aboard the train and tucked them away in an inside pocket in her dress.

Should she look for a hotel? Try to find Mr. Collins's store?

No doubt he was frantic about Charlotte and the baby, but couldn't he have sent more direct instructions?

If this had been Calvin, a young woman alone wouldn't have made it off the platform without multiple offers of help. But this wasn't Calvin, and as she left the station, no one even seemed to notice her.

Outside, horses and wagons bustled past. She held her satchel in one hand and smoothed her other hand down the front of her dress, trying to calm the butterflies that took flight.

The store.

She needed to find the store, and then Mr. Collins would give her further instructions. Like where to find lodging.

She went back into the station, feeling a fool, and waited behind three people before taking a turn at the ticket window to ask the attendant the location of the Collins's Leather Goods store. She knew they lived above the store, because she and Charlotte had commiserated about street noise during their visit to Calvin.

Repeating the directions in her mind, she set out on foot. Darkness was beginning to fall, and she wrapped her coat close to ward off the evening's chill.

Twenty minutes later, her feet were aching and her arms as limp as noodles from carrying her bag such a distance, but she rapped neatly on the door of Collins Leather Goods, as the store had closed for the night, and the door was locked. The storefront was sandwiched between two other stores—also closed—and she didn't see any other way inside. Her feet throbbed, and she didn't want to walk all the way down the sidewalk to see if there was a back entrance.

She didn't bother to disguise her curiosity and stared unabashedly in the store windows on either side of the central door. Mr. Collins had arranged boots neatly on a white tablecloth. Just boots. Their price tags were hidden beneath each pair instead of displayed atop them like her father insisted on at home.

That was a neat trick, no doubt designed to invite interested parties inside to find out the price—and to give the shopkeeper the chance to make a sale. Perhaps she could find some good in this trip, though she wouldn't be there for Janie when her sister returned. But maybe this was a chance to learn some tricks that would help the store.

When no one answered her knock, she banged. The evening's chill was seeping down the back of her coat.

The street was empty except some sort of eatery on the corner, where light and voices spilled out onto the street. A shudder of unease slid through her.

She banged again. Did Sheridan have a hospital? If Mrs.

Collins had been in danger during her delivery, could they be there?

If the Collins's weren't at home, what would she do? She didn't know anyone else in Sheridan.

Finally, she saw movement inside the store. A shadow moving behind the counter. A candle flared, lighting Mr. Collins's face, and she sagged with relief.

"We're closed," he called out.

"Mr. Collins!" she cried, afraid he would leave her out here.

Thankfully, the light moved closer, and she got an even better look at him through the glass.

He'd been a consummate professional in Calvin, but now he wore shirtsleeves, and his hair was slightly mussed.

"It's Liza Bennett," she said through the glass, because he still hesitated and probably couldn't see her with the flickering candlelight reflecting against the darkened glass.

"Liza!"

She heard his relief through the door.

He fumbled with a set of keys and bobbled his candle before he got the door open.

"I'm surprised to see you," he said. "I expected a return wire from your father. Come in, come in."

She followed him through the dark store, careful not to bump against anything. Then through a storeroom and up a narrow set of stairs, where he opened a door and ushered her into a cozy apartment.

She stepped into a small, open kitchen with a potbellied stove and a narrow table with two chairs. The sitting area was beyond it, though its sofa was covered in white cloth diapers. Hopefully clean.

A doorway was open. It must be their bedroom, and a thin voice called out. "Who was it, William?"

He strode to the door, motioning her to follow him. "Just the person we needed. Liza Bennett."

Liza left her satchel in the sitting room and peered into the bedroom. A lamp on the bedside table gave off enough light that she could see how very pale Charlotte was against the bedsheets. A small cradle rested beside the bed, where a dark head was visible among the swaddled blankets.

One of Liza's friends from home, Verity Campbell, had had her first child last summer, so Liza knew better than to make a peep.

"Oh, Liza." Charlotte's eyes welled with tears, and a momentary panic gripped Liza by the throat. Liza went to the bed and exchanged a gentle hug with her newfound friend.

At Charlotte's insistence, she sat carefully on the end of the bed, her skirts nearly touching the cradle.

Mr. Collins stood in the doorway, shifting on his feet. He looked uncertain, as if he had no idea what to do with her.

"I insisted William wire your father," Charlotte whispered, clutching Liza's hand. "The birth was...not easy." Even now, she let out a tiny gasp and pressed her hand to her midsection before shifting in the bed.

Liza didn't know whether to jump up or to stay.

"I'm so grateful you came," Charlotte whispered. Her eyes filled again, and she laughed at Liza's wide-eyed stare. "The doctor said my emotions will stabilize in a few weeks." She gave a soggy hiccup. "I hope so."

"I'm not a nurse," Liza whispered, terrified Charlotte was going to ask her to stay and look after the baby.

But it was Mr. Collins who said quietly, "We can't afford to close the store, not for a week or longer while Charlotte recovers. Your father spoke highly of your skill with customers and with the ledgers, and we'd be deeply indebted to you if you'd run things downstairs while I stay with Charlotte."

She must rethink her opinion of Mr. Collins. He'd been all business while in Calvin. But watching him now, it was obvious he cared deeply about his wife.

"I'll be available should you have a question without a simple answer," he said quickly when she didn't immediately respond.

"I'm here," she whispered. "I'll mind the store for you. But today had been a long day. Where will I stay?"

Charlotte's eyes widened. "Of course. William, you must take her over to Maisey's." To Liza she said, "Maisey was a friend of William's mother. She has one daughter and a large house. She rents out her spare room, and I know she'll welcome you."

15

Janie's trip to visit Aunt Myrtle was cut short when Auntie M's pen pal got sick. Myrtle bundled Janie on the train home and made her own arrangements to travel to New Jersey.

The three-week-long visit had been a badly-needed distraction. But every mile the train traveled toward Calvin seemed to make the voices in Janie's head louder. *Hussy. Seductress.*

She couldn't focus on the book in her lap. She stared out the window, but the scenery passing didn't catch her interest either.

At the stop in Cheyenne, passengers disembarked and boarded. She watched the activity absently.

And then Nathan Bingley boarded the train.

He'd entered the car from the door in front; she sat near the rear, which gave her a clear view as he looked for a seat.

She wanted to sink into the floor. Or maybe hide her face in the book currently resting in her lap. But she sat frozen, unable to look away.

He looked pale, drawn. Pronounced lines around his eyes made it seem as if he might be ill.

His eyes skated around the compartment. There were several empty seats—including one next to her.

Please God, don't let him sit there.

His eyes met hers. He stopped in the aisle, one hand clutching a seat back.

He nodded slightly. And then sat, facing away.

Nearly half a train car separated them.

If she'd held out any hope that he'd want to rekindle their friendship when he returned to Calvin, it was obliterated in that moment.

He'd seen her and chosen to sit elsewhere.

Her hands shook as she opened her book again. She stared at it without seeing.

She felt near tears as the conductor moved up the aisle, checking tickets. She considered asking if there were any available seats in the next car. With still a day and a half of travel along this line, perhaps being out of Nathan's sight would calm her nerves.

But the words froze behind her lips, the conductor passed by, and she was stuck.

She should be relieved that Mr. Bingley hadn't taken the seat next to her. If he had, she'd have had to speak to him.

But the thought was small comfort.

The morning dragged, minutes seeming like hours, hours like years.

Several times, she heard a wracking cough from Nathan's seat. It was bad enough that she found herself lifting her eyes, no matter how fiercely she told herself to ignore the man.

Lunch was a quick stop at a Harvey House. She was jostled by passengers as she disembarked the train. The mess hall was crowded and noisy. She tried not to look for Nathan but did anyway. She didn't see him anywhere. Had he stayed on the train?

What food she could force down lodged in her stomach like lead.

She determined to board a different passenger car—there were two—after the quick meal, but she was near the back of the crowd, and by the time she'd gotten to the platform, she was in danger of missing the train completely. The whistle blew, blasting her ears with sound as she stepped onto the train.

Nathan was there, still in his seat midway up the car.

She sank into a seat nearest the door. She'd get a blast of hot, dusty air each time they stopped, but she didn't dare try for something closer to the man who didn't want her.

The clickety-clack of the rails lulled her into a drowse during the heat of the afternoon. But a loud hacking cough woke her with a jarring start. Nathan.

The conductor moved through the compartment, announcing the next two stops. They were coming up on Cottonwood Cove.

The town where Albert and his mother lived. Where she'd been treated with such contempt over what had been an innocent mistake on her part. She'd been so distraught that she couldn't eat. Couldn't leave the house. And Mama had convinced Papa to uproot the entire family to move to Calvin.

As far as she was concerned, they couldn't pass by quickly enough.

Nathan coughed again.

Was it her imagination, or was his cough worsening? The dry hacking sound had turned wetter.

As a child, Kitty had once come down with croup. She'd nearly died from the sickness. Janie could still remember being awake in her bed into the middle of the night, watching Mama tend Kitty. Being so afraid she would die.

Nathan's cough was beginning to sound just the same.

. . .

NATHAN SHOULD'VE STAYED in Cheyenne and found a doctor.

His stubbornness might be the death of him. The cough that he'd developed in St. Louis had worsened with each mile, and now he felt as if his lungs were filled with the smoky, sooty air from the car's boiler. Each breath burned. Chills wracked his body.

He'd lost two seat mates. No doubt his worsening cough had scared them off.

The conductor called for a stop, but the fuzziness in Nathan's head made it impossible for him to understand the words. Was this a stop for a watering station, or a town?

Janie was on the train. If he could marshal his strength, perhaps he could walk back to her and ask for her help. She was a kind soul, wasn't she? She might overlook that awful letter he'd sent and help him.

But his neck felt rubbery, like it wouldn't support his head, and he had to lean back against his seat.

It had grown dark outside, and he strained his eyes trying to see through the reflection on the window. If there was a town out there, it was small enough that he couldn't make out any lights from this distance.

Another bout of shivers wracked him, and he closed his eyes, trying to rally the strength to do something to help himself.

And then there was motion next to him. Someone sat on the seat beside him. A *she* someone, because her skirts brushed his knee.

He pried his eyes open. Through vision now gone hazy, he saw hope. He smiled. "Dearest Janie." The breath he'd drawn to speak the words burned his throat.

Instead of returning his smile, she frowned. "Are you—?"

"Ill," he announced cheerfully. She was here to save him, and he hadn't even had to ask. "Caught something just before I left my sister in St. Louis. It seems to be getting wor—" Another bout of coughing took him, and he ratcheted up in the seat, doubling over as it stole the very breath from his chest.

This one was the worst yet, and he braced with hands on his knees as he tried to catch his breath through burning lungs and throat.

The train began to slow with a squeal of brakes, the change in motion throwing him off balance. Janie braced his shoulder.

She was kinder than he deserved.

He was probably smiling at her like a dolt, but she was frowning again, this time her face nearer as she settled him back against the seat.

She touched his forehead with the back of her wrist, her skin cool and refreshing against his.

"You're burning up." She didn't sound happy about it. She almost sounded angry. Was she angry?

He realized his eyes had closed, and it was more difficult to pry them open this time.

The conductor yelled "Cottonwood Cove" from the front of the car, and Nathan winced at the harsh sound.

"You've got to get off the train." Her voice was faint, as if he was hearing her through a fog, and he smiled again, his eyes falling closed.

He meant to ask her to help him, to take him off the train, but his voice emerged garbled.

He passed out.

"Nathan."

The man's head had lolled back on the seat again, and he didn't respond when Janie spoke his name.

The train rolled to a complete stop, and several passengers moved toward the door. It opened, and cool evening air whooshed into the cab.

With her hand on his arm, she felt a shiver wrack Nathan's body.

He needed a doctor. There hadn't been one in Cottonwood Cove three years ago, but perhaps there was one now.

Regardless, he couldn't stay on this train. He almost hadn't been able to draw breath after that last bout of coughing.

She looked around for help, but the other passengers were studiously avoiding looking at them, possibly afraid they'd catch whatever he had.

If no one would help, then it was up to her. She couldn't just leave him like this. What if he died?

She had a debt to repay. He'd once braved the floodwaters for her. Surely, she could brave one town for a night. Even if the town had betrayed her once before.

"Last call," the conductor was blaring out the door to the platform.

"Wait!" she called out.

She collected both of their satchels from their feet and roused Nathan by grabbing his upper arm. He moved slowly, but she finally dragged him to his feet. He immediately weaved.

She moved closer, and he hummed, as if he were enjoying her closeness. The way he'd smiled when she'd first sat down in the seat beside him... His entire face had lit. And she didn't know what to do with the emotions his expression had stirred up in her.

Now she needed him to move, so she slid her arm around his waist. His arm came around her shoulders.

He was burning up with fever. She could feel heat radiating off of him through the suit jacket and her light shawl. Her satchel banged against her hip, throwing her further out of balance.

The conductor saw their approach and moved out of the way so they could disembark. Nathan stumbled on the last step to the platform and nearly toppled the both of them.

The train blew, the whistle drowning out any other sound. Smoke curled around them, and Nathan coughed again, bracing one hand on this thigh. She fought to keep him upright.

They needed to find a place to settle him. Three years ago, there hadn't been a hotel in Cottonwood Cove, but she knew where the boardinghouse was. It was only a few blocks.

With Nathan's weight dragging them both down, she wasn't sure whether they could make it that far on their own.

This late in the evening, the town's sidewalks would have rolled up. Only one other person remained on the platform, and he walked away before Janie could call out, leaving her and Nathan alone on the windy platform.

What had she done?

She'd disembarked in Cottonwood Cove. If Albert or his mother found out she was here... They might do violence to her. Edna had threatened it enough times.

She couldn't think about that right now. Nathan's breaths were coming even rougher, sounding more wet. He needed a bed and some steam. She hoped that was all he needed.

He'd rescued her once. Now it was her turn.

The moon was only a sliver and the streets were shrouded by leafy trees overhead. The darkness would've been frightening if she weren't so worried for Nathan.

With each step, he seemed to lean on her more heavily. They had to stop twice as he lost his breath to his coughs. Once, he wheezed so badly that she was sure he would suffocate. Fear surged. All she could do was pray.

A light remained on in the boardinghouse. Perhaps the proprietress expected the occasional evening traveler?

Janie held her breath as she knocked at the door. Her heart pounded with more than the exertion of toting Nathan here. If the proprietress recognized her, if she wouldn't allow Janie in... what would they do?

The door opened a crack.

"Do you have a room for the night?"

Janie didn't know the older woman. Her eyes narrowed slightly. Janie waited for recognition, but none came.

And Janie was worried enough for Nathan, frightened for his very life.

Words that she hadn't planned rushed out of her mouth. "My husband is ill, and we need a room."

16

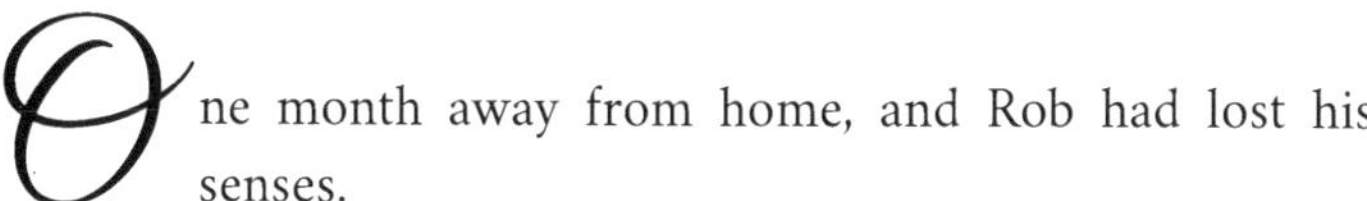

One month away from home, and Rob had lost his senses.

His first Sunday back at the little Sheridan church, and he'd been caught by Maisey Matthews and somehow wrangled into a supper invitation at her home. He'd lost his touch at avoiding matchmaking mamas. Or maybe he'd wanted to prove Liza wrong, even if she'd never know.

He should be on the ranch. His foreman Charlie had done well managing while he'd been gone, but he'd come home in time for summer branding, and he'd barely had a breath of time for anything else.

Tonight, he'd wrangled Charlie into coming to town with him, because Maisey had included him in her invitation and because Rob was too chicken to go alone.

Maisey opened the door to them with a warm smile, but it was the woman sitting on the parlor sofa who drew his notice and brought his whirling thoughts to a halt.

"Miss Bennett." He reached for his hat to sweep it off his head, but then remembered evening had fallen, and he hadn't worn it inside.

Maisey gave him a sharp look, and there was an edge to her tone that hadn't been present before. "You know our guest?"

His throat was suddenly dry as he took in Liza's hair styled up behind her head, the snap in her blue eyes before she averted her gaze, the fold of her hands on her lap. Tiny lines framed her mouth. She looked tired.

She looked beautiful.

He cleared his throat. "I had the pleasure of meeting Miss Bennett in Calvin."

Her chin lifted, and her eyes seemed to contradict him, though she didn't protest his statement aloud.

He registered Charlie at his shoulder and moved into the room to allow introductions for his foreman.

Maisey's daughter, Priscilla, sat opposite Liza, and he didn't know where the greater danger lay. If he sat next to Priscilla, it might give her, and her mother, the wrong idea.

But sitting next to Liza...

She was a danger to his equilibrium.

His indecision won him a spot standing between the two sofas while Charlie sat on the edge of the sofa next to Liza.

"What brings you to Sheridan?" Charlie asked.

Liza opened her mouth to answer, but Maisey spoke over her.

"Miss Bennett is working in one of the shops while her friend recovers from childbirth."

Liza glanced his way briefly, only a flash of her eyes, and then her lashes lowered against her cheek. "I believe you met Mr. and Mrs. Collins."

"Yes." The man had made an awkward introduction at the barn raising.

Charlie asked Liza something else in a low voice, and Maisey turned to Rob. "If you ask me, Mrs. Collins would've done better to ask her local friends for help."

No doubt Liza could tend the store without requiring additional training. Liza had come to help her friend.

Liza was *here*.

"Don't you think my Priscilla's new gown is the loveliest shade of rose? It compliments her complexion just so, don't you think?"

"Yes, of course." His ears grew hot. Priscilla's face flushed a shade to match her dress.

Another knock sounded, and Maisey turned for the door, leaving him to breathe a sigh of relief at her momentary absence. Voices sounded in the vestibule.

Charlie's head was bent toward Liza as she said something so softly that the rest of the room couldn't hear.

Their proximity caused something ugly to roar through Rob.

ANOTHER MOTHER and daughter joined their party.

Liza probably shouldn't take pleasure in watching Rob's discomfort grow.

At least she wasn't the only one uncomfortable. It was more than obvious she was an unwanted guest at tonight's event. Watching Rob scramble for words gave her something to smile about and eased Maisey's pointed conversational redirections and sharp glances.

Maisey had rented her a room as a favor to the Collinses. Liza left the house early each morning, before mother or daughter arose, and had mostly returned to a covered plate left on the stove—the remains of what they'd eaten for the evening meal.

Tonight, William had insisted she close up shop early. Liza doubted he'd noticed her exhaustion. At home, Papa only allowed her in the store during the afternoon hours, but she'd worked open to close all week long. Perhaps Charlotte had encouraged William to let her go early. On the lunch hour, she usually slipped upstairs to visit her friend. Charlotte was improving, but slowly.

And Liza's early arrival had interrupted Maisey's supper preparations. She hadn't understood the woman's black look at her presence until the first knock on the door.

There was to be a dinner party.

And she wasn't supposed to have been invited.

She would have made some excuse to escape to her room, except she was ravenous and the smells of roast and stewed vegetables had glued her feet to the floor.

It didn't mean she wouldn't feign a headache after the meal and escape. She didn't know whether she could be polite to Rob for so long.

Rob was Nathan's friend. Nathan had broken Janie's heart. She could only force so much civility.

Plus, there was the issue of George Wickham. Cowboys worked long hours during the summer months, and Liza hadn't seen him in weeks, but she couldn't forget what Rob had done to him.

Maisey introduced Mrs. Kimball and her daughter, Cynthia, and the group adjourned to the formal dining room.

The table had been set with china and a lace tablecloth, and Liza was rewarded to see Rob's grimace before he hid the expression behind a polite smile.

Maisey swept to the head of the table, but with an odd number of guests, Liza held back, waiting to see where the woman would seat her.

The two men hung back as well, which meant that when Maisey pointed Liza to the seat at the center of the table, Rob was right there to push in her chair. His fingers brushed her shoulder, and an unexpected shudder went through her. She hid it by shaking out her napkin and placing it on her lap.

Rob sat beside her, Priscilla on his opposite side. Charlie, who she'd learned was his foreman, sat across from her, flanked by Mrs. Kimball and Cynthia. Maisey sat at the head of the table.

Charlie was pleasant and polite. When Maisey had been distracted greeting her other guests, he'd leaned in and asked for her protection against the matchmaking mamas. His bluntness and humor had put her instantly at ease.

How was it that Rob could collect such decent friends when he himself was difficult? Even now, she was intensely aware of him at her elbow.

Thc meal had been served, and she'd just eaten a decadent bite of roasted potato when the man beside her spoke.

"How is your family?"

She chewed and swallowed before answering. "As well as can be expected. Janie is currently on a visit to my aunt." She refused to ask about Nathan.

"How long will you be staying in Sheridan?" Charlie asked. She turned his direction, enjoying the way his eyes crinkled when he smiled.

Had Rob smiled once since his arrival?

"A week or two more. Charlotte is getting stronger every day." She took another bite, only to be mid-chew when Maisey addressed her.

"Your mother must be very brave to send you so far away from home."

The way she said it, the words didn't sound like a compliment to Mama.

Liza forced a smile. "I'm afraid Mama was against it. Papa was insistent that I come."

"Still, it is such a distance to travel for a young woman alone. I would never allow Priscilla..."

"From what I've seen, Miss Bennett is plenty capable," Rob said without looking at her.

What—?

Charlie grinned across the table at her. "A high compliment from my friend."

Maisey glared, her lips set in a thin line.

And Liza was still so stunned she didn't know what to say.

She redirected. "This is an excellent meal, Maisey."

ROB'S CHANCE TO converse civilly with Liza was rapidly dwindling.

Maisey and Mrs. Kimball had gone into the kitchen to prepare coffee and a treat while the younger folks had been ushered into the parlor to chat.

Priscilla and Cynthia sank onto one of the sofas, smoothing their skirts. Liza moved behind the couch, toward the front hall.

"I'm quite tired," Liza said. "I think I might retire."

Rob hadn't entered the room completely yet and moved on instinct to intercept her.

Charlie stood behind the sofa where the other two women sat, and Rob caught his raised brows.

"You can't go up yet," Priscilla said. "We're going to play a card game."

"I must be at the shop early," Liza said, though she smiled a genuine smile at the young woman. "Besides, this way it'll be evenly matched."

That's what he was afraid of.

But that wasn't all of it. He wanted her to stay. He wanted her to keep talking. Smiling.

He cast about for something to say, some way to dissuade her, but it was Charlie who came to his rescue. "You haven't told me yet how the boss spent his time in Calvin. I'm surprised he didn't return with a wife."

Charlie's words were pointed, though Liza seemed to miss their meaning. Charlie had somehow tracked his feelings. Rob squinted slightly at his friend.

"I wasn't aware he was looking for one," Liza said in that teasing manner he so enjoyed.

He hadn't been.

She glanced at him, her mouth curved slightly. And even though her humor was at his own expense, he couldn't be offended, because her smile was somehow becoming dear to him.

"Rob attended a town dance with the Bingleys on his first night in Calvin, but he refused to dance, though there were plenty of girls without partners."

She and Charlie leveled identical expectant glances on him. Charlie had stepped closer, and the two young women on the sofa seemed to be lost in their own conversation.

What excuse could he give?

He directed his words at Charlie, though he meant them for Liza too. "You know I'm more at home with cattle than new acquaintances."

Charlie's eyes twinkled. With how often Rob sent him into town for supplies on the ranch's behalf, the foreman knew it was true.

But it was the pinch of Liza's lips that made his stomach swoop low. "Then perhaps tonight will be a good exercise for you." She spoke low and nodded to the two young ladies now glancing curiously in their direction. Maisey and Mrs. Kimball came through the kitchen door, each carrying a silver serving platter.

"Good night, gentlemen."

Liza's soft laugh followed her up the stairs, and his gaze lingered long after she'd disappeared.

"You didn't mention Liza Bennett when you told me about your exploits in Calvin."

Charlie's words emerged from the darkness. Rob was a little surprised he'd waited this long to bring it up.

The men rode side-by-side on the rutted road, having already left the bustle of Sheridan behind. The moon was half-full and provided plenty of light for their ride down this familiar lane.

Rob had just started to feel as if he could breathe again, the cinch that had been tightening his chest since stepping foot onto Maisey's front stoop finally loosening.

But Charlie's easy question tightened it right back up.

"I seem to remember plenty of discussion about a *Janie* Bennett," Charlie said when he didn't answer, "but not one mention of Liza."

"There's nothing to tell." It wasn't completely true. It seemed he'd done everything wrong while in Calvin, culminating in that final dance where her words had stung immeasurably. Because Wickham had *charm* and Rob did not.

"But you want there to be?" Charlie was too perceptive for his own good.

Rob considered kicking his mount into a gallop and leaving his friend and foreman behind, but wouldn't that action reveal more than it hid?

"The situation is... difficult."

"More so than your inability to communicate with a pretty girl?" Charlie chuckled at his own wit.

Rob didn't take offense. He hadn't been joking when he'd

said he was more comfortable with the animals. If you watched their behavior, animals always told what they were feeling.

Women did not.

"Her family is—I already told you about her mother when we spoke of Nathan. The woman has no sense of decorum and makes it plain as day that she's only interested in matching up her daughters with whoever has the most wealth."

"Ah, yes. And your family is the perfect example of decorum."

Rob snorted. It was true. His sister Danna dressed like a man and had a man's job and, thanks to her supportive husband, didn't worry about what others thought.

"You and I both know that women like Priscilla and Cynthia would never last on the ranch." Women who enjoyed lavish parties and visiting with friends on a daily basis were often sorely disappointed.

The ranch required everyone to work hard, to pull together. There wasn't much time for visiting, and though they often turned a nice profit, there were hard years when the crops didn't make it, and spending frivolous money on parties wasn't something Rob enjoyed.

"You sure Liza is like them? She seems a hard worker. You said she was capable."

So he had.

Rob had noticed her exhaustion, though. He'd seen it in how she carried herself, the tired lines around her mouth. Were the Collinses taking advantage of her giving nature and working her to the bone in their shop?

He thought of Liza and the joy she exuded in every moment —in conversation with her family, friends, and customers.

He imagined that joy disappearing.

After a long pause, he said, "And if she did accept my suit?

What if I drove her away the way I did Danna? I couldn't keep my own sister happy."

Charlie knew his history. Knew that Danna had almost died from exposure and a broken leg because of him.

"Your kid sister was grieving. And so were you. You're older now. Wiser."

"Maybe in the ways of ranching. Not so much with matters of the heart."

Because if he were, Liza would already know his feelings for her.

17

Janie had been able to secure a room in the boardinghouse. With her faux husband.

She had insisted on taking a smaller room downstairs, near the kitchen.

The proprietress, Mrs. Killen, had told her there was no doctor in town. And she herself was exhausted and going to bed, but Janie could have access to the kitchen.

It was better than nothing.

Mrs. Killen disappeared before Janie'd even hauled Nathan over the threshold. Arms, shoulders, back, everything aching, she dropped her satchel on the floor and took two steps before he took a shuddering breath and slumped forward.

Luckily, the bed was there, and Janie released him.

He sank heavily into the mattress, eyes closed.

Why had she lied? She was still trembling from the falsehood.

Had he heard? On the way from the train station, he'd drowsed in and out, but at least his feet had kept moving.

What would he think of her for telling the lie? The situation was desperate, and she'd panicked.

But would he see it as a necessity or as a manipulation on her part? Especially after the letter he'd sent her.

She backed away from the bed, stared at the man on it. His eyes were closed. He was asleep, which was good, because... Oh, what had she done?

The situation was ten times worse because they were in Cottonwood Cove. The best she could hope for was for Nathan to make a speedy recovery so they could escape from town first thing in the morning. Before anyone she'd known before saw her, recognized her.

She dared brush his hair away from his forehead. She needed to bring his fever down immediately.

She found a pitcher of cool water and a washcloth on the stand beneath a large window, next to a wardrobe. She wet the cloth and then rolled Nathan onto his back before she laid the cloth over his forehead.

He still had on his suit jacket and boots. She flushed as she took them off. It seemed too intimate for their situation.

Of course, he'd seen her in her nightgown and wrapper when she'd been convalescing on his ranch. She supposed this made them even.

She left the door open when she went to the kitchen. His uneven, shallow breathing worried her.

She stirred up the coals in the stove and put a pot of water on to boil, being as quiet as possible so as not to wake the rest of the house. There were no medicines to be found in the cabinets, and she didn't dare wake Mrs. Killen. She remembered her mother giving Kitty steam treatments. Surely that could ease Nathan's cough, too.

Finally, she took a large towel from beneath the sink and returned with it, the now-boiling water, and the bowl.

Nathan moaned when she touched his shoulder. His head rolled on the pillow.

"I need you to sit up."

He didn't even crack his eyes open.

"Nathan." She shook his shoulder. "Sit up."

He made a sorry attempt to push up on his elbow. She had to put her arm around his shoulders to help him. Then she put the bowl in his lap and the towel over his head and poured the hot water carefully into the bowl, sending steam up to be trapped in the towel.

She kept one hand on his back. "Breathe in as deeply as you can."

She kept him there for as long as he could bear, then took the bowl, set it on the table beside the bed, helped him lie back down. He shivered as the cooler air from the room hit his damp skin, and she pulled up the blanket from the foot of the bed to cover him.

He smiled such an open smile that it caused her insides to clench like a fist. "Thank you, dear Jane."

She went about returning the bowl and the now-cool water back to the kitchen and making preparations to do it all over again.

She was shaking.

Making a fool of herself over the man, that's what she was doing.

No doubt his easy affection was due to his illness. Fever caused delirium, didn't it? Obviously, he was suffering from it.

Only her heart didn't seem to understand. Its rapid fluttering and the thrum of her emotions meant one thing.

When he recovered, she was going to get her heart crushed all over again.

. . .

Nathan's body was betraying him. His lungs ached and burned, and he alternated between being as hot and dry as a cowboy fire during branding and shaking with cold and chills.

Every time he woke in the dark of night, Janie was there. She forced him to drink cool water. She held him when coughs wracked his body.

Once, after she'd insisted he breathe in the steam yet again, he pulled away the towel covering his head to find she'd fallen asleep sitting beside the bed, her head resting on her arm on the edge of the bed.

Wisps of her hair had come loose and curled around her face, damp from her chore. Her lashes were a dark smudge against her cheeks and her mouth wore a small moue of exhaustion.

It would be so easy to fall for her. She was beautiful, inside and out. After the barn raising, he'd been uncertain of her feelings. Rob had confirmed that she'd seemed indifferent.

But did one get off of a train in an unfamiliar town to spend the night nursing someone they didn't care about?

He was exhausted and still having trouble breathing. He hated to wake her, but... "Janie," he whispered.

She roused with a small shake and quickly jumped up from the chair when she saw him looking at her.

"Here. Let me take that. You lie back down."

It'd been years since someone had bossed him around like that. His mother was the only one who'd ever cared that much. When he'd been thirteen or fourteen, he'd been sick with a high fever. He could still recall her bossy, no-nonsense attitude as she'd worked to heal him.

And here was this creature behaving the same way. It was lovely. He found himself smiling even as he drifted off to sleep again.

The next time he cracked his eyes open, Janie was sleeping

curled in the chair, directly in a shaft of morning sunlight beaming through the window. Her hair was slipping its pins, and part of it already tumbled down her back. A strand rested against the curve of her cheek.

Sounds reached him, someone banging around in a kitchen nearby, humming a hymn if he wasn't mistaken.

His throat ached, and he couldn't help a raspy cough. The sound of it was much improved over last night.

Janie moved, her head tilting as she shifted and then settled again.

He was breathing easier but still felt like his chest was a saddle someone'd cinched two notches too tight. His bones ached, but he thought the worst of the fever must be past.

He didn't dare sniff himself, afraid he stank of sick sweat.

He reached for the water glass on the bedside table. His arm felt like it weighed more than a newborn calf, and after he'd slaked his thirst, he sat back against the headboard, weak from just that much.

He wouldn't be able to travel today. Maybe tomorrow, if he was able to sleep and if his cough continued to improve.

His movements woke Janie, who hummed slightly and pushed her hair out of her eyes. Her eyes widened, and she went pink when she realized he was awake. She straightened in the chair, and he saw the faint lines on her face where it had been pressed onto the chair.

"Good morning," he said easily.

She nodded, turning slightly away as she reached up to pull the pins from her hair. The mass of golden curls spilled down her back, and he found himself breathless from more than his illness. She was quick to sweep up the tresses and twist them in a move she must've practiced hundreds of times before she pushed the pins back in, leaving her hair in a bun at the back of her neck.

She went to a pitcher and bowl on a stand across the room and splashed her face with water before drying it with a towel.

When she finally turned back to him, her hands were clasped in front of her, her shoulders straight, and her spine ramrod straight. She wasn't smiling.

She hesitated at the end of the bed. She'd been much closer last night, but now the distance he'd sensed between them at the barn raising had returned.

Only... with the fevered realizations he'd had last night, he wondered if the distance was only a mechanism to protect herself, her feelings. He was almost sure she cared for him.

"How are you feeling?" she asked.

"I'm quite improved." He tried a smile. "Thanks to you." He wanted to lift a hand to salute her, but his strength remained sapped, and his hand fell back to the bed before it'd reached chest-height.

Her eyebrows came together in concern, and she glanced at the door before moving to his bedside. There was a slight hesitation in her movements as she reached out to touch his forehead with the tips of her fingers.

"I think the fever is gone," he said. "But I must confess, I feel as weak as a baby."

Somehow, the idea of being stuck with her for another day wasn't a trial at all. He felt quite cheerful about it.

Then he had a thought. "Are your... Your parents will be worried about you, won't they? If you aren't on the return train today? I suppose you could go ahead without me. I'll be fine in a day or so."

She glanced at the door again, and a flush rose in her face. "I'm afraid if I leave..." She stumbled over whatever she was trying to tell him. "You see I had to...I told..." She pressed both hands against her cheeks and whirled away, giving him her back.

A memory niggled at the edge of his consciousness. Something from the depths of his fever last night... It came to him in a flash.

"You told the boardinghouse woman we were married."

She whirled back, and her expression was apologetic. Almost guilt-ridden "It was a tiny lie. It would've been a scandal if she knew we weren't married. There's no doctor in town, and who would've taken care of you in the night?"

He held up one hand, his lips twitching at the waterfall of words from the woman who was usually so composed.

"I don't see any harm in it," he said.

Her eyes widened, and she sat on the end of the bed suddenly, as if all her energy had been sapped. "You aren't angry?"

"Angry that you spent all night boiling water so I could breathe? And then covering me up when my chills overtook me? That you worked yourself to exhaustion to help me—" He broke off in a fit of coughing, thankfully one that didn't last nearly as long as any last night.

She went to the nightstand and poured the last of the water from the pitcher into his glass.

His eyes snagged on her hands.

Her right hand moved to cover her left wrist, but not quickly enough. There was a raw, pink spot on her skin. A burn? A fresh one. His heart thrummed hard.

"A simple thanks for what you did last night will never be enough."

Her eyes were luminous as she stared at him. He couldn't read what resided in their depths. Shadows, or... hope?

Or maybe he was still fighting feverish imaginings.

She pressed her folded hands to her midsection.

"Then perhaps we are even," she said quietly. "Because I felt the same way after you pulled me from the creek."

18

Janie browsed the meager selection of fresh fruit at the Cottonwood Cove grocer. It was early afternoon, and Nathan had grown hungry, though he'd only admitted it when pressed.

Mrs. Killen had allowed them to take breakfast in their room. Janie had apologized for making noise in the night and the small mess she'd made, but the woman had brushed it off, which was a kindness.

She'd served breakfast and set a time for supper. They were on their own for the noon meal, if they wanted it.

Nathan had insisted he didn't need her to wait on him, but she knew he needed nourishment if he meant to recover completely. She was relieved that his fever hadn't come back, but his cough lingered.

She'd gone out on the pretense of sending a wire home, so her folks wouldn't worry when she didn't get off the train in Calvin today. That much was true, but she would also purchase a small meal of cheese and bread and fruit.

She'd made it to the grocer, the line of shops along First Street as familiar as her own reflection, with a jangle of nerves.

No one had accosted her. No one had shouted names, not like before. Maybe she'd been forgotten.

She could only hope.

But as she selected two oranges and moved to the selection of fresh bread that she knew the local baker supplied each morning, the tinkling bell above the door jingled, and a familiar figure entered the store.

Claudine, who'd once been a good friend. Until the end, when Albert had thrown her over and his mother had spread her accusations around town.

Janie ducked her head, quickly choosing a loaf from the top.

"Janie? Is that you?"

She forced her chin up, though a tremble passed through her legs. "Hello, Claudine. It's been a long time."

"It's been ages! What are you doing here?"

Janie wished she were better at discovering people's motives. If she were Liza, she'd know whether the undertone in Claudine's voice was simple surprise or something more sinister.

"I was traveling home by train when my companion—my husband—became ill." Last night, in her worry for Nathan, the lie had slipped easily off her tongue. Today, she stumbled over the words, afraid Claudine would see right through her, afraid there would be another scene. *Shameful.*

"You're married!"

"Y-yes." She chose the first chunk of cheese she touched and then moved to the counter, where the grocer waited to tally what she'd chosen.

Claudine came closer. The heat in Janie's face intensified. All she wanted to do was escape.

She tried for a smile but was sure it emerged more like a grimace. "In fact, I have one more errand, and then I really must return to him."

She snatched up the foodstuffs and left the store, for the first time in her life not caring whether her actions were rude.

She wanted to hop right on the next train and disappear from Cottonwood Cove altogether. What if Claudine told Albert or Edna that she was in town? What if there was a scene?

It would be her worst nightmare playing out all over again. This time with Nathan present to witness it.

Oh, she wanted to escape so very badly!

But she couldn't forget Nathan's weakness, the rattle of his cough. If she left him behind, and his fever returned, what would happen to him?

Where the sunshine earlier had left her feeling hopeful, after the encounter with Claudine, she felt like an insect beneath the heel of a child, in danger of being crushed. Was there someone she knew behind every storefront? Did they all still believe Edna's awful accusations? Were they laughing at her—or worse, judging her?

She was shaken and near tears by the time she reached the telegraph office near the center of town.

She'd already composed what she wanted to say to Mama. She carefully left out any mention of Mr. Bingley, knowing Mama would spread gossip about the two of them around Calvin like wildfire.

And then she rushed to return to the safety of the boardinghouse. Surely, no one would come looking for her, demanding that she present her husband like a train ticket, prove she was really married.

Why should they care, anyway?

Perhaps it was only her wild imagination, playing tricks and seeing menace where none existed.

When she reached the dappled shade of the boardinghouse street, she attempted to draw several calming breaths. She didn't want Nathan to know she was upset. She could imagine nothing worse than the man who'd already shown he wasn't interested in her to find out what had happened here in Cottonwood Cove.

Something had happened while Janie had gone out to fetch the foodstuffs they'd devoured in the room.

After resting all morning, some of Nathan's strength had returned. He'd gotten out of bed and paced to the small window to peer out the lace curtains to the street.

He saw nothing sinister, nothing interesting, in fact. Only a quiet street and a row of unassuming houses.

But something had spooked Janie while she'd been out. Had someone accosted her?

She'd been quiet, more so than usual, and distant after the meal, sitting in her chair as far across the room as she could be from him. She'd opened her book and focused on the words, but she hadn't turned a single page. Was she simply avoiding speaking to him?

As the afternoon wore on, boredom and his continued weakness had him dozing restlessly. He awoke, hot beneath the quilt. He flipped it away. He'd stayed fully clothed beneath in deference to Janie.

She was still sitting in that chair, but now she was staring at the wall, at nothing. She didn't seem to register that he was awake. But as he watched, a silver tear slipped from her eye and rolled down her cheek. She brushed it away.

Janie was upset. Whether from whatever happened earlier or from being with him, he didn't know. *He* was the reason she was here. She'd gotten off that train to help him, and now she was crying.

He sat up in the bed, suffering a rush of wooziness at the

action. He braced against the bed with one hand and raised the other to clutch at his forehead.

"Nathan!" She was instantly out of the chair and by his side.

He waved her off. "I'm fine."

But she still reached out to him, her palm cool against his forehead and her opposite hand steadying his shoulder.

She did care about him. Her actions over the past day proved it, no matter what Rob thought.

And Nathan couldn't help a grin.

"I'm fine," he repeated. "I just sat up too fast." A short bout of coughing belied his words, but the food and inactivity, not to mention being off the sooty train, had done wonders for his constitution today.

Being with Janie had caused the improvement in his attitude.

She wrinkled her nose as his coughs subsided, and that made him grin again.

He stretched his legs out toward the floor. "Do you think Mrs. Killen will serve supper soon?"

The kitchen had become noisy again while he'd dozed. Scents of warm bread and some kind of roasting meat must be wafting beneath the door, because his mouth was watering. And he wanted to shake Janie out of the funk she'd suffered this afternoon.

He was filled with new hope. Janie *did* care about him. And when they returned to Calvin, he'd do something about it.

"If it's supper you want, I suppose I should freshen up a bit." She turned to stand before the looking glass above a wooden dressing table.

Freshen up. Yes, he'd love a bath, but that might have to wait. He had a fresh shirt in the small satchel, and he tried his best not to watch Janie as he searched through the small bag for it.

It was a losing endeavor.

With each pin she removed from her hair, the golden mass slipped farther down her back until it was all down. She used a brush from the table in long, sweeping strokes. Each one hypnotized him more and more.

She was so beautiful.

She caught his stare in the mirror and flushed.

He ducked his head, focusing again on his satchel on the floor. "Mindy and I aren't close. I've never seen a woman put up her hair. I've never been married. I was engaged once." As the words fell from his mouth, surprise surged through him. He hadn't meant to reveal that.

Now it was his turn to go hot.

He rubbed the back of his neck. Opened his mouth to take the words back, but instead, what emerged was, "She threw me over for someone with a better salary than a cowboy's."

A moment passed before she spoke. "I'm sorry." Janie's whispered words were impetus enough to look up.

Her hair was still down, her hands and the brush rested in her lap. In the mirror, her eyes were trained on him, soft and filled with compassion.

"Ironic, then, that I received the attorney's letter about my inheritance only weeks later." He didn't mean for bitterness to seep through his words, but now that he'd started, he couldn't seem to stem the flow. "She heard about it and returned, begged for my forgiveness."

He looked away from Janie's gaze in the mirror. He'd been so lonely, so desperate for someone to love him, that he'd wanted to believe her motives were pure.

He'd told her this much. He might as well tell the rest. "Rob helped me discover her true motives. She didn't love me—probably never had."

And he'd been blinded by wanting to believe the best of Hildy.

"What a terrible ordeal," Janie murmured. "I don't understand how people can be so cruel."

She'd gone back to brushing her hair, and he couldn't catch her eye in the mirror now. Her words... there had been more than compassion in her tone. It had sounded like... empathy.

As if she'd been a victim to some kind of cruelty as well.

"I can take comfort in the fact that there are genuine people in the world." He meant the words as a compliment to her, but again, she wouldn't meet his eye.

Whatever had happened today, he wanted to ease it for her.

As she finished her hair, leaving the locks in a braid tucked under into a bun, he moved behind her in the mirror. From this close, it would be awkward if she avoided his gaze. She didn't. The shadows in her eyes remained, and he wanted them gone.

"You look beautiful," he said simply. "Shall we go to supper?"

It's pretend. All of it is pretend.

Janie repeated the words to herself silently as she and Nathan left the boardinghouse the next morning. His hand rested at the small of her back, and he carried her satchel.

Last night at supper, he'd been conscientious, serving her first from the platters on the dinner table, leaning close in conversation. They'd remained in the common parlor, chatting with another couple who'd been staying overnight.

Nathan was charming and kind and...

It was all an act.

She mustn't forget it. When they got back on the train, Nathan would go back to being a friend—or less.

He'd severed the blossoming relationship between them with his letter.

But... what he'd shared with her before supper last night hadn't been in public. His wounds from the woman who'd broken his heart had been a gift given only to her.

She wanted to believe it meant something. But perhaps he was only telling her so she would understand why he couldn't be involved with her.

The only reason he was behaving so kindly now was to keep up the charade she'd started. And maybe gratitude for her help while he'd been sick.

But oh... it was tempting to believe that he wanted her again.

When they walked down the street and he reached for her, drawing her hand into the curve of his elbow, she wanted to cling and never let go.

When they clambered up onto the train platform, he smiled warmly before leaving her to go to the ticket agent.

On the night they'd arrived in Cottonwood Cove and he'd been so deathly sick, she'd had the passing thought that he would break her heart all over again. Perhaps it wasn't his fault, though. It was her and the hopes and expectations that leaped to life in her breast.

She wanted to be loved by him. Ached for him to return the feelings that had blossomed since their first dance.

She was a fool.

The platform was nearly empty. Only three other individuals waited for the morning train. It couldn't come quickly enough to suit Janie. She wanted to go home, where Edna's accusations weren't waiting around every corner.

She stood near the tracks, comforted by the low rumble of Nathan's voice as he purchased their tickets. She couldn't help turning to watch him. The man drew her.

He caught her looking and grinned.

And then, she watched in horror as a familiar figure in a stark black dress ascended the stairs to the platform and bee-lined straight for Nathan.

Edna. No!

"Excuse me, young man?" Her voice carried easily over the open platform.

Nathan was too polite to ignore her, though Janie wished he would.

She couldn't look away from what was unfolding.

She wanted to run, but run where? She had to board the train to get back home.

She wanted to shout to Nathan and tell him to ignore whatever Edna would say. She didn't dare.

All she could do was watch.

"Are you acquainted with that young woman?"

Nathan smiled as he followed Edna's pointing finger to Janie. He had no idea what was coming.

"Yes, that's—Janie. My... erm, wife." He stumbled over the words, just as she had, no more comfortable with the lie than she'd been.

Edna narrowed shrewd eyes on him. "I'd heard she was back in town—"

"Yes, I'm afraid I was very sick two nights ago, and we were forced to get off the train."

Edna interrupted Nathan. "I just wanted to warn you, in case no one else had. She's a lying trickster. And a hussy."

Nathan's smile faded as he stared at Janie. "I think you must be mistaken."

"No mistake. She tried to coerce my boy, my Albert into marrying her. She seduced him and almost ruined his reputation and then lied about it when I confronted her."

Janie couldn't bear to see Nathan's confusion or the judgment that would surely cross his face. She turned her back, staring at the empty train tracks and the prairie beyond.

Wind blew strands of her hair into her face, causing her eyes to water. That must be it.

The train whistle blew from far off. She could see the black-and-red engine and colorful painted cars approaching in the distance, a line of gray smoke rising from the steam. The whistle blew again, momentarily muting the conversation behind her.

"—been a mistake," Nathan was saying.

"There was no mistake," Edna said sharply.

Oh, there had been. Janie had made the most monumental mistake in falling for Albert in the first place.

"If she was innocent, why'd her father up and close their store? The entire family left town in the night, like thieves, the lot of them."

It hadn't been like that at all, though Nathan had no reason not to believe Edna.

The train rushed closer. Its brakes squealed now, and the whistle tooted again, ending Janie's chance to hear anything else Edna had to say about her.

The train pushed into the station on a rush of warm air. Janie closed her eyes against an onslaught of tears.

She definitely didn't want Nathan to see her weep. But she was unsure whether she could hold back her tears for the entire ride back to Calvin.

Her only intention in getting off that train with Nathan had been to help him through his sickness. But with Edna's false accusations, would her lie to get them into the boardinghouse seem more sinister?

Would he think she'd done it to trap him into a relationship he didn't want? He'd made it clear enough in his letter that all he wanted from her was friendship.

This was a disaster.

And she still had to face him to get on the train.

She blinked rapidly, her pride refusing to show how deeply she'd been affected by what had just happened.

The train chugged twice before coming to a complete stop. The doors opened, and the conductor shouted, "All aboard!"

She sensed Nathan beside her, from the corner of her eye saw the curve of his shoulder and the brim of his hat.

She stumbled on the smooth metal step to the train, and he took her arm. This close, she couldn't avoid seeing his face.

He didn't smile. His face was an unreadable mask.

Her heart thundered in her ears.

If only the compartment were full, that there weren't two seats together.

But of course, there were plenty of places for them to sit.

Nathan followed her into the empty row and sat beside her, arms crossed over his chest.

She couldn't help the tremble of her mouth, could only pray he hadn't seen.

She almost wished he would ask. Speaking of Albert was painful. There had been no seduction on her part. Albert had charmed her. He'd come courting, and she'd fallen fast. They'd met secretly. He'd told her he wanted to marry her and pushed for more physical intimacy than she'd been comfortable with. That's when Edna had burst in and spewed her accusations against Janie.

More had followed, to everyone Edna knew. She'd seemed to forget, or ignore, Albert's part in their assignation.

Janie didn't like talking about it. But the silence that stretched between her and Nathan was more painful than revealing her naivety and shame.

Especially when it stretched for a minute. Five minutes. Ten.

And then an hour.

She kept her gaze on the window. Scenery passed, but she didn't see any of it.

Any hope she'd felt on the short walk to the train station was obliterated. Gone.

Nathan would never see her the same way again.

Hussy.

Seductress.

She was the only one who heard the sound of her heart breaking.

19

A dreary, rainy afternoon had kept the store empty most of the day. Several days had passed since Maisey's dinner party. Charlotte had felt well enough to venture down to chat with Liza for a good half hour earlier, and Liza had gotten the chance to hold baby William. He'd snoozed tucked up against her shoulder. William Senior was sequestered in the storeroom, catching up on accounting reports where he'd fallen behind.

Nuzzling her cheek against the softness of the baby's cap of downy hair had brought such a strong desire for a baby of her own that Liza had to blink against the sting of tears.

For much of her childhood, she'd dreamed of becoming a mother. Imagined what her husband might be like, how many children they'd have.

And then she'd told Edna Rockwell that Janie and Albert had snuck away, and everything had snowballed from there. She'd caused Janie's anguish, caused the family to lose all the faithful customers from Cottonwood Cove.

Now she quashed any dreams of a family for herself. She

would be content to find Janie a match and to make good on the family's store. It was the penance she deserved.

Soon enough, the baby had fussed for his mama, and the two of them had returned upstairs, leaving Liza alone in the store to outlast the gloomy afternoon.

Liza was standing on a stool using a duster to attack the high shelves behind the counter when the door opened on a blast of wind and rain.

She startled, clutching the nearest shelf to steady herself as she glanced over her shoulder.

Rob Darcy came inside, water dripping from his hat and slicker. The door closed behind him, shutting out the sound of distant thunder, a reminder of their adventure on the plain weeks ago.

She stared, sure her mouth hung open as he took his hat off and swept one hand down his face. His hair was rumpled and dark.

He stood there, dripping on the floor and returning her stare.

The moment seemed to stretch. The tick of the clock on the shelf behind her magnified, the only sound other than her own breathing and the drips falling from his clothes to the floor.

"Mr. Darcy." She stepped off the stool, careful not to lose her balance on legs that suddenly felt weak and wobbly.

Her movement seemed to galvanize him.

"I was afraid you'd have returned home."

His words rang loudly in the empty store, or else his presence had discombobulated her to make it seem so.

"I plan to catch the train on Tuesday." Charlotte was much recovered, and Kitty's birthday was in ten days. Mama had sent a letter that she was wanted at home.

"Tuesday," he repeated.

She couldn't imagine what he might've needed from the shop that he'd braved the rainstorm for.

He stared at her in a way that made a blush rise in her cheeks. His presence caused a flash of memory from the afternoon Mr. Wickham had come into the store, the way he'd looked at her.

Somehow, Rob's look was more intense.

She didn't know how to feel about it. She hid the duster behind the counter and pressed both hands against the countertop.

"Was there something specific you came in to find?"

Unless she was mistaken, her words caused a glint in his eyes.

Rob clutched his hat between his hands. Surely he was ruining the brim. "No, I—" He cut himself off and shrugged almost helplessly.

"Liza?" Mr. Collins called from the storeroom. A little relieved, she heard his footsteps approach and turned to see what he needed.

He emerged carrying a sheaf of papers that he tapped idly with a pencil.

A surge of wind and the scent of rain brought her head back around in time to see the back of Rob's slicker as he ducked outside, back into the storm.

She was left with her mouth hanging slightly open.

"Was that—?"

"Mr. Darcy," she told Collins. "He appeared suddenly and then left just the same way."

"Huh." But Collins seemed only absently interested. "Do you remember seeing a box of brass belt buckles?"

She followed him into the back to help locate it. She couldn't help sending one more look over her shoulder to the door.

How strange.

The entire episode stayed with her all day and into the evening, long after she'd retired from a quiet supper with Maisey and Priscilla.

She wished Janie were here to talk to. And possibly giggle about Rob's actions. What had driven him to visit the store? It was a conundrum, and she hated not knowing!

Was Janie still grieving the loss of her relationship with Nathan?

Liza needed to see her sister, to make sure she was all right. Tuesday couldn't come soon enough.

After two days of storms, the weather in Sheridan cleared, and they experienced a balmy summer day.

Mr. Collins relieved her for a lunch break, and Liza took her sandwich and walked along the city streets, window shopping.

Mr. Collins had paid her a tidy sum for all her help with the shop, and she could surprise Mama and the girls with some baubles. Maybe she'd find a pretty bonnet for Janie.

She paused on a street corner, satisfied to watch the bustle of people on the street. A carriage rolled along, drawn by a pair of matched black horses. That first evening, she'd been frightened of the city's very bustle. And there was a part of her that missed home, missed the quiet streets of Calvin and her shared bedroom above the store.

But she was glad she'd come. Glad to have had this experience.

And she hoped that she could take some of what she'd learned working in Collins's store home to make Papa's store a success.

She still didn't know what to make of Rob's appearance. She

couldn't fathom why he'd come, and it bothered her, not knowing.

She was pondering his possible motives when someone stopped on the street corner next to her and cleared his throat.

She looked up into Charlie's smiling face.

"Charlie!"

He tipped his hat to her. "Hello, Miss Bennett. You sure looked like you were woolgathering."

She laughed, unable to keep from returning his warm smile. "I'm afraid you caught me." She held up the remains of her sandwich, then tucked them into a cloth napkin from her pocket. "I'm enjoying one of my last breaks for lunch, doing a little window shopping, and I lost track of myself."

"Then perhaps it's a good thing I saw you and stopped to say hello. I'd hate for you to end up hopelessly lost. Would you allow me to escort you back to the Collinses' store?"

She took his arm, and they fell into step. For some reason, being on his arm made her think of Rob. Once again, she realized that Rob was surrounded by decent friends. How did someone like him ended up connected to people like Charlie and Nathan?

"Do you find Sheridan much different from home?"

"Oh, yes." She allowed him to escort her around a couple coming from the opposite direction on the sidewalk. "There's much more traffic. It's much noisier. Of course, my family hasn't always lived in Calvin."

"No?"

"No. We moved there about three years ago." She looked up at him. "How long have you worked for Rob?"

He squinted slightly as if considering his answer. "It's been... five years now. No, six. He's a good boss. Generous. Not afraid of hard work. Why do you ask?"

He looked down at her, and though she hadn't intentionally done so, she found her nose was wrinkled.

"You have a different view of him?"

She shrugged. "I've seen firsthand that he can be high-handed and unkind."

He shook his head. Perhaps they would have to agree to disagree on the subject of Rob's character. "The thing with your sister excepted—"

"What thing?"

Suddenly, he turned red and clamped his jaw shut.

She stopped short, forcing him to turn and face her on the sidewalk. "*What* thing?" she demanded.

He grimaced. "I don't suppose there's any chance you'll forget I said that."

She shook her head slowly.

He sighed. Took off his hat and swept his hand through his hair.

She swallowed against the sudden knot of tears in her throat. "He sent Nathan away, didn't he?" And in doing so, broke Janie's heart.

"I don't know all the details." But Charlie's words were confirmation enough.

"How dare he meddle in their relationship," she seethed, stomping away. She didn't take Charlie's arm again, though he followed her.

She had a mind to find Rob and tell him exactly what she thought of his interference. Not that she knew where his ranch was located, or had a horse or cart. In fact, if she never saw him again, that would be all right by her.

Charlie kept pace with her easily. "I didn't mean to… he didn't want you to find out."

No doubt. If she'd done something so despicable, she wouldn't want anyone to know, either.

"Don't worry, Charlie," she said. "It isn't your fault that your boss is a deplorable human being."

"Aw, Miss B…"

They'd reached the corner just down from the leather shop and she nodded curtly. "Thank you for the walk. It was most enlightening."

She left him there on the corner, looking forlorn as if someone'd stolen his horse.

If she never saw Rob again, she'd count herself lucky.

LATE MONDAY NIGHT, Rob waited until Liza had exited the leather shop, sending one last goodbye over her shoulder.

He shouldn't have left this until the eleventh hour, but the summer storms had flooded one of the ponds on his property and knocked down a fence. He'd spent the two days since he'd last seen Liza up to his chin in mud and with very little sleep.

Urgency had sent him into town. He had to know if there was a chance Liza returned his feelings.

Before she left Sheridan.

She took several steps down the sidewalk before she caught sight of him and stopped short. Her eyes widened, then narrowed.

"Hello, Liza."

She pursed her lips, and for one wild moment, he expected a smile.

She frowned. And didn't return his greeting.

Was she laughing at him after he'd burst into the shop and then acted like an awkward teen, too afraid to speak to the girl he fancied?

He was still kicking himself for that performance.

"I thought I might escort you back to Maisey's."

That put her into motion again. She strode down the side-walk. "That's not necessary."

Her words gave him pause. But he had to know. He fell in beside her, his long strides matching her pace easily.

He extended his arm to her, his pulse pounding loudly in his skull at the blatant invitation for her to touch him.

She ignored it.

He knew she'd seen it, had seen her eyes skip to him and then away.

A sense of foreboding rolled over him, but he soldiered on. He had one chance to get this right.

He cast about for a way to ease into the conversation.

She wasn't making this easy. Maisey's house wasn't more than a fifteen-minute walk. Maybe ten, at the rate Liza was marching down the street.

"I…" He cleared his throat. "I think we make a fine match."

She stopped short, the movement abrupt as she whirled to him.

"*What?*"

Her incredulous reaction wasn't quite what he was expecting. If he'd said the same words to Priscilla, she'd be looking at him with joy and hope in her eyes.

Liza was almost... glaring at him.

"I think we make a fine match," he repeated.

Her brows bunched over her expressive eyes.

He *was* considered to be an excellent catch.

"I can't stop thinking about you," he said. The words he'd rehearsed on the ride to town stuck behind his breastbone. It wasn't easy for him to reveal his feelings to another, not when his and Danna's relationship had been strained for so long. "I know there are issues with your family." He meant with the store. He knew they'd fallen on hard times, and certainly he'd help, if he could. "And that marrying me would mean moving from Calvin, but I'm... I think we can work through those things. Would you consider... marrying me?"

"No."

Her answer was swift as a sucker punch.

And he couldn't have predicted the humiliation and hurt that speared through him. A hot knot rose in his chest, an ache that wouldn't be assuaged as he pressed his hand to his ribs.

"How can you expect me to consider you after what you did to Janie?"

Her words took him aback.

But she wasn't finished. She advanced on him now, her hands on both hips. "You sent Nathan away, don't deny it."

He shrugged. "Why would I deny it?"

She made a sound that was half-growl, half-scream, then threw up her hands and stalked away.

And, fool that he was, he followed. Obviously, she didn't understand.

"She didn't fancy him."

She glared at him.

"She didn't," he defended. "I watched them closely at the barn raising, and she gave no sign of interest."

"I think I know my sister better than you," she said scathingly. "Janie is shy."

He shook his head. "Not shy. Indifferent."

She whirled on him again, this time pointing her finger in his face. "You don't know what she's been through."

She seemed to catch herself. She inhaled deeply, her nostrils flaring. She tucked her chin in. "Trust me on this. Your friend broke my sister's heart."

Her words hit a soft place inside. He hadn't meant to hurt Janie. Liza hadn't elaborated, but there was obviously something more to Janie's bashful nature.

Her chin came up, her eyes flashing. "And then there's Mr. Wickham."

Just hearing the name made him see red. "Mr. Wickham," he repeated, voice gone icy.

She stood her ground. "He told me all about what happened between you."

No doubt a pack of lies. But Liza had believed him, judging by the fire in her eyes.

"There's nothing you could say to me that would make me want to marry you."

Liza had judged Rob and found him wanting.

And the blow to his pride was too much to bear.

He nodded once. "I'm glad there's no question of what you really think about me."

Something flashed behind her eyes, but he was past caring.

"Good day, Miss Bennett."

He whirled and strode away.

20

Rob stared into the semi-darkness the next morning. On horseback, he sat on the roadside just outside of town, trying to decide whether he was on a fool's errand. Dawn lightened the sky to slate gray. His horse had its head lowered and was alternately nibbling at roadside grass and dozing.

He had spent a sleepless night replaying the conversation with Liza.

He hated that she believed him cold. That she believed whatever accusations Wickham had leveled against him.

Grandfather had been an early settler in the area. A smart investor who'd bought up homesteads from folks who'd failed to make a living on the tough land. Grandfather had been one of the founders of Sheridan.

Rob had been raised here, and the community knew him, respected him.

Had he taken it for granted that Liza would see him the same way? They didn't know each other well.

And he had split up Nathan and Janie. That much was true.

But it was his pride that was wounded even more than that.

She thought Wickham a better man than him.

That stung.

Was his pride even worth salvaging? Should he let her go?

He'd vacillated the hours it'd taken him to ride to town and now fingered the letter he'd spent an hour slaving over in the darkest hours of night.

It revealed more of himself than he'd shown to anyone except his sister.

Did he even want to share it with Liza after she'd thrown his proposal back in his face?

Something inside had driven him to write it and was driving him still to deliver it to her. He knew she'd be at the train station this morning.

It came down to the fact that he didn't want her to go back home thinking so low of him.

And that's why he spurred his horse toward town.

Satchel in hand, Liza stood on the platform as the passengers for this stop disembarked.

The conversation with Rob last night had left her unsettled.

She could've sworn she'd seen a flash of hurt cross his face when she'd refused him. But—

She couldn't even fathom his claim that he had feelings for her. How could he care about her, care enough to want to marry her, when they didn't even know each other?

The passengers disembarking slowed to a trickle, and the conductor leaned out of the nearby passenger car. He cupped one hand around his mouth and yelled, "All aboard!"

But before she'd taken a step forward, a voice called her name. "Liza!"

She whirled, her satchel banging against her knees.

Rob strode through the crowd, edging around an older

passenger bent over a trunk. His broad shoulders sent that same shudder of awareness through her.

And the awareness seemed stronger, now that she knew he had feelings for her.

But he didn't smile, and there was no warmth in his eyes as he neared. He slowed before stopping just out of arms reach.

"Here." He extended an envelope to her.

She took it automatically, her fingers numb.

He turned and strode away without another word. She watched his broad shoulders and dark head for too long.

The conductor called again, and she couldn't miss her train.

She boarded, sending one last look across the sea of faces on the platform. Rob had disappeared.

Seated next to an older woman in a large straw hat, Liza settled her satchel at her feet.

The station blurred as they left it behind, and then plains stretched out to the Laramie mountains in the far distance.

Rob's letter rested on her lap. Though it couldn't be more than two sheets of paper and the outer envelope, it felt weighted with expectation and emotion.

Did she dare open it? No doubt it would be a scathing set down.

But her curiosity compelled her, and she slid one finger beneath the flap of the envelope.

Dear Liza,

I will not repeat my proposal or the sentiments that so disgusted you. I want only to set straight the two matters that caused you to question my character.

Mr. Wickham came to work the ranch for my grandfather, and they became close. When Grandfather died, he left to Wickham a section of land and enough cattle to start a herd. The land and cattle would've provided for Wickham for years, but instead of working, he asked me to buy him out. I did, and I believe he gambled away most of the cash. Last year, he returned to the ranch and asked for a job. I gave him one as a cowhand.

At Christmas, my sister Danna and her husband came to visit. They brought a teen girl that's like a sister to Danna along with them. Katy is an orphan, impressionable. Only seventeen. Wickham flirted with her until she fancied herself in love with him. I will spare you the details, but he attempted to take advantage of her. When he was found out, I threw him off the ranch. Katy was devastated by what almost happened.

Liza folded the letter in her lap with hands that she found were trembling. She stared out the window, unseeing.

How terrible for a young woman to suffer such a thing. Wickham's account was so different. He'd painted Rob as the bad guy.

But for reasons she couldn't quantify, she believed Rob.

Wickham was a consummate flirt. She'd never imagined he could do something as harmful as forcing a young girl... Maybe he'd learned his lesson after Rob had thrown him off of the ranch.

She touched the corner of the letter. She'd touted Wickham as a man of character and insulted Rob's. That was an unforgivable offense.

She picked up the letter again.

As to the second matter, I genuinely believed that Janie was indifferent to Nathan. If, as you say, her shy nature held her back from showing her emotion, then I ask your pardon. You hinted at Janie having suffered heartbreak. Nathan has too. He won't thank me for revealing it, but he was engaged to a woman who threw him over for another. After Nathan came into his inheritance, she returned, seeking his favor again. He is tenderhearted, as you know. He still had feelings for her and asked for my help in determining whether she really loved him or was interested only in his money. We let it be known that my holdings were even more than his, and set up a time where she and I would be alone together over dessert at a dinner party. She took the bait and turned her wiles to me. Unfortunately for her, her game was up. Nathan was deeply hurt, though he hides it well beneath his jovial demeanor.

When Nathan asked my opinion on Janie's feelings for him, I gave it. Nathan is like a brother to me, and I won't apologize for my attempt to protect him, though I am sorry if my actions wounded Janie.

Yours,

Rob

SHE FOUND her cheeks wet as she folded the missive and slipped it into the pocket of her traveling gown.

She'd known nothing of Nathan's past and had a feeling that Janie didn't either. And she'd severely misjudged Rob.

He might be highhanded, but he'd done what he had in support of his friend.

She'd departed Sheridan. There was likely no way she could repair the tenuous connection that had been between them, fractured so by her callous refusal of his proposal.

She'd made a horrible mistake.

21

The late-summer journey to Montana had been a much-needed distraction for Liza. Auntie Myrtle had returned from her trip to New Jersey and sent for both Janie and Liza.

After spending three weeks with Auntie Myrtle, Liza had learned to think of Rob—of the injury in his eyes those last moments together, his letter, the man himself—every hour instead of every quarter hour.

Even now, she was aware that they'd pass by Sheridan and his property in the next hour or so. Dusk was falling. Maybe if she closed her eyes, she could pretend she didn't know the town was there.

After a month of Liza's quiet attitude and Janie jumping every time a customer entered the shop, Mama had received a telegraph from Myrtle and demanded the two girls take the sight-seeing trip.

Janie had regained some of her color these weeks away, though she remained introspective and refused to talk any time Liza brought up Nathan.

Another few hours and they would be home.

The train braked abruptly, throwing the women forward, nearly unseating them.

"What on earth...?" Liza righted herself, glancing quickly out the window. It was completely dark, no lights of any small town or even a watering station. Why were they stopping?

A gunshot punctuated the air outside the compartment. Then another.

Everyone inside quieted, and fear hung heavy like a cloud. A baby whimpered.

Was the train being robbed?

The train continued to slow, and then there were loud shouts and hoofbeats and another gunshot.

Janie clutched Liza's hands.

"It'll be all right," Liza whispered. An utter lie.

Moments after they stopped, two men with dark hats walked through the compartment, one with a gun held pointed at the conductors back as he marched in front of them.

"Everyone"—the conductor gulped—"get off the train." His voice was so low he could barely be heard, until the man with the gun jabbed him in the back and he repeated his words more loudly.

Questions from the passengers rose in a murmur, rose until the second robber pointed a gun into the air and fired a shot into the ceiling of the train. It left a gaping hole in the wood overhead. Smoke rose from the gun barrel, and no one dared make a noise.

Except the baby who wailed loudly now.

Liza heard a frantic, "Shh!" from a woman who must have been the baby's mother.

"Everyone off!" the second robber growled.

Liza held tightly to Janie's arm as the crowd pushed. She hit her shin on the seat as they were shoved from behind.

Without a platform to step onto, the drop to the ground seemed enormous. None of the men who'd jumped down stuck around to help. They were all hurrying away from the train with the women and children.

Liza had no choice but to jump. Her ankle rolled beneath her as she hit the ground with jarring force. She fell but pushed back up quickly, reaching back up for Janie. Her sister landed with more grace.

They hurried away from the train into the growing darkness and scrub brush.

Surely the robbers wouldn't take the train outright.

But that's what they did, minutes after the remaining passengers disembarked, stumbling into the darkness. The conductor had shouted for them to follow the tracks. But how long would it take to reach Sheridan? They must be two or three miles out, at least.

"We'll be all right," Janie said. "We can make it."

But Liza's ankle throbbed with each step. She didn't think it was broken, but walking on it wasn't helping.

She stumbled once. Again.

Night animals called all around them, and she shivered in terror. How long had they been stumbling in the darkness? Surely it was past midnight now. How much farther to the station?

Every limb ached. Her foot was a white-hot throb. Minutes blurred together.

The night air was cool, and she was chilled through, except for the hot flare of pain with each step.

Time passed. She had no concept of how much. They'd fallen behind the rest of the passengers because of Liza's ankle. The low murmur of voices ahead had grown quieter and quieter.

And then there were galloping hoofbeats and voices rang out. "Hello!"

Panic rose, cutting off her breath momentarily, until another voice carried to her. "It's the sheriff."

Janie sighed, a huge gust of air into the night. "Oh, thank heavens. We're back here!" she called. "Hello!"

But when a rider came closer, the moonlight shone enough to illuminate the man's face beneath the Stetson. It wasn't a sheriff at all.

It was Rob Darcy.

ROB HAD NEVER FELT such thunderous relief as he had when he caught sight of Liza Bennett, her face pale and drawn in the moonlight. He hadn't even known she was among the train passengers.

"Liza!" He was barely aware of her sister beside her as he turned in the saddle to call out to his sister, "Danna, over here!"

He threw his leg over the saddle and slid to the ground. "Are you all right?"

"Liza's foot is injured," Janie was quick to say, though the glance she shot Rob was dark and inscrutable. Maybe it was the bad lighting, and he'd misread her.

He moved toward the two women, horse following close. His boots crunched on the gravel and dirt packed around the railroad tracks.

"I'm fine," Liza was insisting to her sister, but Janie shook her head.

He joined them and put a hand beneath Liza's arm for support. He was gratified when she leaned into him, though it was likely only a sign of her exhaustion and nothing else.

"What're you doing out here?" she asked softly. Her face was aimed at the ground, and he couldn't read her tone to know whether she was relieved or angry to see him.

They hadn't separated on good terms.

With a little distance, he'd realized he could've handled things differently. Was it any wonder her answer had been no when he'd botched the proposal so badly?

Right at this moment, he was glad to see her. Relieved beyond measure that she was unharmed.

Danna rode up, calling a greeting to him. He waved at her with the same hand that held the reins.

Then he answered Liza's question. "The sheriff got wind of the robbery and intercepted the train at the Sheridan station. I'd met Danna and her husband in town, and we happened to be eating in a restaurant near the station when one of the deputies spotted my sister and recruited her to ride out and find the passengers. Charlie's here, too." Somewhere. If Liza wanted the cowhand, Rob would be eaten up by jealousy, but he'd bear it. She'd seemed to gravitate toward him when she'd been in town before.

Danna didn't dismount. "There's one or two folks with bumps and bruises up ahead, but for the most part, they're uninjured."

"Liza's sprained her ankle," he told his sister.

"It's only twisted," she muttered.

"Twisted, then."

Janie was watching the interplay between himself and Liza.

"Rob's spread is closer than the station," Danna said. "The night's almost half gone. You two should stay the night. Chas and I can escort you home tomorrow."

He probably should have thought of offering himself.

"Oh—"

"—yes," Janie finished before Liza could refuse.

Probably she'd been planning to refuse.

"I'm beyond exhaustion," Janie said, "and after the scare tonight, I won't mind traveling with the marshal."

"We don't want to impose," Liza argued softly.

"It's no imposition," he said quickly. "Danna's right, it's closer. You should stay."

Finally, she looked up at him.

And her words from his horrible botched proposal were burned into his mind. *There's nothing you could say...*

"If you'd like," he said belatedly.

He couldn't read her eyes in the dark. Had the corner of her mouth twitched?

"Why should we receive special treatment?" Liza pressed.

"You're injured," he returned. "And... friends help each other, don't they?"

He felt the weight of Danna's curious stare but didn't look her way.

Danna went to fetch Charlie so Janie could ride along with him. Danna and Chas would help get the other passengers to the Sheridan train station and then ride back out to Rob's place.

Liza shifted slightly, and he caught the slightest wince as pain crossed her features. He wanted to ease it.

And remembered how she'd once teased him.

"Don't worry. I won't leave you on foot out here."

Her chin lifted slightly toward him. "Even if it isn't entirely proper for us to ride together?"

She remembered, too.

Charlie arrived and helped Liza into Rob's saddle first, then lifted Janie onto the back of Rob's animal.

They made for home.

He was holding Liza.

He set a slow pace, worried about his horse stepping in a hole in the low light.

And enjoying having her close. She must be exhausted, because instead of sitting ramrod straight, as she had when they'd ridden together before, she rested against his chest.

"Were you and your sister traveling home?" he asked quietly.

"Yes. Our aunt took us sight-seeing in Montana."

"What an unlucky time to be on the train."

She hummed agreement. "I thought Janie might faint when the two gunmen came through our compartment. She was brave, though."

His arm at her waist tightened automatically. "They came through your compartment?"

"They were quite violent." Her voice shook on the words.

Perhaps she hadn't had a chance to process what had happened until now. She'd been in the thick of it. He felt her take a shuddering breath.

And then she sniffled.

Liza, one of the strongest women he knew.

He wanted to gather her close. Wished that he had that privilege, but he didn't.

"No one will see it if you shed a few tears," he said quietly.

Her head moved slightly against his shoulder.

"And I won't tell."

She laughed a wobbly laugh. "It's all finished now. Wouldn't it be silly to cry?"

He heard the hiccup in her voice.

"Not silly." He'd made mistakes with Danna when she was a young woman, hadn't known what to do with her feminine emotions.

He desperately wanted to do better now.

"You're safe now," he said.

And that set her off. She cried softly, one hand coming up to wipe away her tears.

. . .

LIZA DIDN'T KNOW what to make of this Rob Darcy.

The man who'd been highhanded and told Nathan to break Janie's heart was now... sensitive?

Nothing about his hold on her was improper, and settled in the curve of his arm, resting against his shoulder, she felt... protected. Safe.

But she'd rejected his proposal. And no doubt damaged his pride. Just because he was being kind now didn't mean he felt anything for her.

In the middle of her crying jag, she felt him shift behind her. Then he pressed a handkerchief into her palm.

She hiccupped a sob. Was this the real Rob? Would she have been the recipient of more of this conscientiousness if she hadn't rejected him?

A very tiny part of her brain recognized that her thoughts were whirling from an overload of emotion and fear still swirling through her belly.

Her tears eventually dried up to the occasional sniffle, but she didn't relinquish his handkerchief. She fingered the soft fabric.

"We're nearly there."

Rob's voice startled her. She must've dozed off.

A soft murmur from nearby was probably Charlie telling Janie the same thing.

The moon had descended in the sky, and stars twinkled overhead, but it was hard to see anything on the ground.

A sleepy cow lowed. A horse whickered nearby. And a structure rose out of the darkness, a shadow against the starry sky.

"The barn," Rob said. "It's not far to the house."

The barn was massive, rising two stories. From this

distance, she could see a corral and the silhouettes of several horses inside.

There were no farm implements left out. The yard was clean and neat. It was obvious Rob took pride in his operation.

And then they reined in near the long, low ranch house.

It was large, too, made up of logs neatly squared off. Light from a long window on one side of the house illuminated a rectangle on the ground outside.

"Hold on," he said just before he swung out of the saddle. He reached up for her, his hands spanning her waist as he helped her to the ground.

He kept his hold on her as she tested her weight on her injured foot. It pained her, but not like it had when she'd been walking on the rocky, hard ground beside the railroad tracks for hours upon hours.

"It's a little better already." She looked up to find Rob gazing down at her.

The light shone in her face, and she squinted against it, trying to decipher his expression.

And then Janie and Charlie were there, dismounting with a rustle of clothing and a low murmur.

Rob let go of her and moved slightly away. When she wobbled, he steadied her with one hand beneath her elbow. "All right?"

She nodded.

"I'll take your horse, boss."

She couldn't see him in the dark, but she imagined she heard a smile in Charlie's voice. Rob didn't argue as he took the reins and led both horses toward the barn.

"Come inside," Rob said. "Watch the stair, there."

He supported Liza's arm as she followed Janie up the steps to the long porch that spanned the length of the house. A pair of rocking chairs swayed gently in the breeze.

Liza's foot sent another shaft of pain up her leg, and Rob steadied her again.

She was afraid she could get used to his coddling.

"Janie, the door?" Rob asked. "If you please."

Janie pushed through the door into the house, and Liza followed more slowly on Rob's arm.

She almost didn't want to go inside. In the intimacy of the darkness, Rob had seemed... softer somehow.

She was afraid that when they stepped into the light, he'd revert to the caustic, distant man she'd known before.

The kitchen was huge, more than any one person needed.

And then she realized with a barn the size of the one they'd passed, his spread must also be massive. And he'd need cowhands to run it. Hands needed to eat, so... the big kitchen made sense.

A long counter would be lovely for preparing large meals. The stove was large and clean, it's black surface empty of stains. She imagined he must have a large root cellar outside as well, though she hadn't noticed in the darkness.

One lamp was lit and had been shining from the windowsill. A small table beneath a window in the corner had two chairs and would be perfect for enjoying a cup of coffee before the cook started a big meal in the mornings. Through a doorway, she could see part of a darkened room and a long dining table and chairs. Elegant chairs, judging by the cut of the wood on the chair backs.

Rob settled Liza at a chair at the small table and moved away. He took down the lamp and proceeded to light another, filling the room with more light, but she hardly registered his actions, she was so fixed on the simple beauty of his home.

A knot took residence in her throat.

This could've been her home, if she'd accepted his proposal.

Rob brought the lamp toward her, and she swallowed to dislodge the obstruction in her throat.

Janie knelt at her feet.

"Let's get that shoe off," Rob said.

Janie sent him a sideways glance as she reached for Liza's shoe.

"It's really not necessary," Liza said. "My foot is much improved already."

"It won't hurt to look," Janie said. "Just to be sure you don't have a sprain."

Her shoe came off easily, and Janie peeled off her sock as well. There was no swelling, only a small bruise beneath the knob of her ankle. Rob leaned the lamp close enough for both of them to see it, and Liza stifled a hysteric giggle at both heads, dark and fair, leaning close over her foot.

"I'll be right as rain after a good night's sleep." Liza primly settled her skirt back over her foot, hiding it from sight.

Rob looked up at her, their gazes connecting. And holding.

Janie stood, the motion broke the invisible contact.

"I'm sure you're thirsty after your exertions tonight." Rob pointed to an upper cabinet. "There are cups there. Water in the pitcher and milk in the cool box."

He edged toward the dining room and whatever was beyond. "Help yourselves, and I'll make up your room."

Janie was already moving toward the counter.

"Don't—" Liza stifled her initial refusal when Rob's eyes came to rest on her. He'd been so kind to her already tonight. "Don't go to any trouble," she said quietly. "Janie and I can make up our own bed, can't we?"

Janie nodded, her head in the upper cabinet.

"It's no trouble." He held her gaze, but she couldn't decipher what was in his eyes.

He disappeared into the house.

Janie filled two Mason jars with cool milk and brought Liza's to where she sat at the table.

Her eyes were wide. "Have you ever seen such a beautiful kitchen?" she whispered.

Liza swallowed the boulder that had risen in her throat again. She cleared her throat. "No, I certainly haven't."

22

Liza woke early to sun streaming around the gingham curtains.

Beside her in the big bed, Janie slumbered on.

Rob had showed them both to a room at the back of the house soon after they'd finished their milk. He'd left before Liza had been able to form a protest.

She suspected he'd given up his own bedroom.

The room was large and had its own stone fireplace built into the outside wall. It was far too warm to use it, but she could imagine cold winter nights snuggled in the large bed, with a fire crackling nearby...

No, she shouldn't imagine such things. His kindness didn't mean a return of his feelings.

She must remember that.

She desperately wanted to peek in the heavy oak wardrobe in the corner, just to glimpse what she could of Rob's life. A Stetson rested atop it. His Sunday best?

The bed had four large carved posts and the most comfortable feather tick. She'd fallen into a deep sleep almost immediately, worn out from the robbery and all the walking and their late-night ride.

But now she felt rested.

She waited another quarter hour, but Janie still didn't wake. Liza slipped from the bed and splashed her face with water from the basin. She wrinkled her nose at having to don yesterday's traveling dress. She'd left her carpetbag on the train and could only hope it had been taken off at the Sheridan station.

She tiptoed through the quiet house, irritated to find all the bedroom doors closed.

But the parlor... She'd glanced inside last night, but the room had been dark.

Now she slipped in. A pair of lovely brocade sofas faced each other over a braided rug. Another stone fireplace would make this the most enjoyable room during the winter. Two large windows flanked the fireplace. The view overlooked the sweeping land, the barn, and the corral. A heavy sideboard displayed pretty china dishes.

Next to one window stood an upright piano.

Liza couldn't resist. She tiptoed across the room and touched the keys gently, not hard enough to play the notes. They were smooth and cool beneath her fingertips.

Out the window, she caught sight of two riders coming to the yard. She didn't know the first, but the second... It was easy enough to recognize Rob's tall, muscled form. He rode with easy grace, confident in the saddle.

The two men rode into the barn as she watched, unable to tear her eyes away.

"Do you play?"

The voice from behind startled her, and in her fright, Liza pressed down on the keys, eliciting a discordant noise from the piano. She winced even as she turned to face Rob's sister, who stood in her marshal's trousers and vest. “Sorry. I didn’t mean to frighten you.”

"I’m a little jumpy after yesterday.” She took a breath and smiled. “I do play a little. I had lessons when I was a young girl. We've never had enough space to own one."

A soft clacking on the wooden floors came from another room and quickly grew louder. A small... animal?

"I think we've woken him up," Danna said with a wry smile.

A brown puppy raced into the room, ears flopping and tongue flying out of the side of his mouth.

"Watch out," Danna said as the puppy beelined for Liza. "He's a bit of a rascal."

The pup jumped, placing its two front paws on Liza's knees, its tail wagging so hard it might've fallen over.

"Oh, my." Liza lowered herself to the floor and folded her legs beneath her. The puppy tumbled into her lap, nosing into her skirts and then kicking its feet in the air.

Liza rubbed its head, scratched its ears, and was rewarded with a warm scrub of its tongue. The puppy laid its head on her thigh, tail slapping gently against her foot.

She scratched his ear again. "Oh, you are a dear, aren't you?"

"Don't be fooled," Danna warned. "He'll bite your—"

The puppy had already grabbed her sleeve in his razor-sharp teeth and was attempting to play tug of war.

"Oh, you!" Liza used her other hand to disentangle herself with a laugh. She distracted the puppy with a tummy rub, resulting in him lying on his back on the floor, tongue lolling.

Liza smiled down on the dog. It clambered back into her lap, this time resting its chin on her thigh and relaxing. "As a child, I always wanted a dog. But as I said, our rooms above the store are too small."

Just remembering how many Christmases she'd spent

hoping for a puppy beneath the tree sent a pang through her now.

Danna watched her avidly. "I'm afraid my brother is a little too fond of his dogs. He has two adult shepherds that sleep in the barn, but he's brought this pup inside." She shook her head as if she couldn't understand it.

An outside door opened and closed, and footsteps came from the direction of the kitchen.

Moments later, Rob appeared in the doorway beside Danna.

His brows rose when he saw Liza on the floor with the puppy draped across her lap. He nodded to her.

She rubbed one hand across the dog's back. He was so soft. "Good morning."

She didn't know why she felt shy. Somehow the intimacy of riding on his horse with him last night—and maybe the softness in his eyes this morning—had changed something between them...

...for the better?

Liza's stomach gurgled noisily, and a blush rose in her cheeks.

Danna grinned. "Brother dear, I think you'd better feed your guest."

She shook her head quickly. "Oh, I don't want to—"

"—put me out, I know." But Rob said it with a smile that sent her stomach spiraling in a way that had nothing to do with food.

"The next train doesn't leave until late this afternoon," he went on. "And I wouldn't like you to starve in the meantime."

"Besides, Chas'll be hungry too," Danna said.

Liza set the puppy on the floor and stood. The ornery thing chased her boots as she followed the other two into the kitchen.

Rob looked back at her. "How's your foot?"

Her foot. She'd barely thought of it today. "Better."

Rob was both relieved and dismayed that Liza had recovered. Relieved that she was uninjured and dismayed that this meant she was free to leave. If she'd had a sprain or a break, he might've been able to convince Janie that the sisters should stay over for a day.

When he'd come into the house and seen her loving on his puppy, Brownie... The sun had been shining through the window just so and gilding her hair with golden tones. The simple joy on her face had made him want to bring back that expression again and again.

Things had ended badly between them before. But this morning, she seemed open and warm. He had maybe three hours to use what little charm he possessed to try and woo her.

And his sister was looking on. He'd confessed to fancying Liza, but Danna didn't know about the botched proposal. He would take that to his grave, if he could.

In the kitchen, he put the puppy outside and then rolled his sleeves to his elbows and washed up at the basin. He couldn't help his awareness as Liza passed by him to do the same, so close that their shoulders almost brushed.

"You're cooking again?" Liza asked when he pulled a cast iron skillet from its hook above the work counter.

"You don't want to eat anything that Danna's had a hand in preparing." He took a slab of bacon from the cool box and rifled through the drawer for his best knife to slice it.

Liza looked to his sister, probably expecting a rebuttal or exasperation, but Danna only shrugged. "I'm a horrible cook. Chas and I would've starved early on in our marriage without Katy. She was orphaned, and now she lives with us. We left our toddler with her back in Calvin. Good thing, after the wild ride last night."

Rob began cracking a dozen eggs from the basket on the counter, ones he'd brought in from the henhouse earlier. He was utterly surprised when Liza settled in next to him at the counter, rifling in the cabinet until she located the flour and then fetching the milk.

"It doesn't seem fair for you to have to cook for all of us," she murmured when he questioned what she was doing. "I can mix up some biscuits."

Danna sat at the nook table, and with Liza's back to his sister, she didn't see when Danna waggled her eyebrows.

Liza glanced at Rob, and he could only shoot a glare at his sister and her antics.

Chas banged in the back door, offering a hello and a nod to Liza and giving Danna a smacking kiss on her cheek.

Rob and Liza worked well together. It was almost like a dance the way she moved around him at the stove as he flipped the bacon. Her shoulder brushed his thigh as she bent to place the pan of biscuits in the oven.

When he'd removed the last piece of bacon from the pan, she was there to exchange the plate of bacon for his bowl of eggs, offering him a soft smile.

He could get used to this.

"Did your parents build this house?" she asked Danna, settling one hip against the counter.

Danna grinned. "Rob built it."

Liza looked to him curiously. "Maybe it's an impertinent question, but—have you been married before?"

Danna outright laughed at that.

Heat fused in his face. "No."

"It's just that"—Liza gestured around—"this is a large house for a bachelor."

That heat remained in his face. "Um..."

"He built it for me," Danna said.

"It was a mistake," he muttered to the scrambling eggs.

"A mistake?" Liza asked.

Danna laughed again, and even Chas chuckled.

Liza looked between them, maybe trying to understand the interplay between them.

"Danna was married before," he said. "Her husband was sheriff in Calvin and was killed in the line of duty."

"And when Rob heard that Fred had died," Danna said, "he started building this house, thinking I'd move back home."

"Only my sister is the most independent, stubborn woman I'll ever know." He tipped his egg spoon at her. "And the best marshal I know."

Danna flushed with pleasure. "I don't know about that last part."

Chas nodded his agreement. "She's smart as a whip."

"Well, I'll be doing my investigating from behind a desk again." She focused on Rob. "I'd meant to tell you later, but... we're expecting again."

He stood in stunned silence for a beat, then felt a wide smile cross his lips. He left his spoon in the pan and moved to sweep Danna up into a hug. "Congratulations. Another little terror to spoil."

She laughed into his shoulder. "No one is as much a terror as you when we were children."

"True." He let his sister go and clasped Chas's shoulder. The other man was beaming, watching his wife with a smile.

"Congratulations," Liza echoed softly. She'd moved to the stove to stir the eggs, making sure they didn't burn when he'd abandoned them.

Rob reached for the spoon to take over for Liza, unable to stop his smile. Another niece or nephew. He couldn't wait.

Liza's return smile, small though it was, lit him up. Had she ever smiled at him so softly before?

Chas and Danna spoke together in low tones, and Liza hovered nearby. She was probably waiting for him to mess up their meal, but he'd made enough eggs to know what he was doing. Not that he was complaining.

"So…" Her voice was gentle when she spoke. "You decided to construct the ranch house even though your sister wouldn't move home?"

He poured the scrambled eggs into a waiting bowl on the counter. "The project was already started." He shrugged. "I thought it would make a good place to raise a family." His face went hot again.

And he really didn't want to talk about his marriage prospects with the one woman he really wanted. "Danna and I grew up in a tiny cabin closer to the foothills," he rushed on. "I needed the bigger barn and so it seemed like the smart thing to do."

And then he was able to stick his face into the oven's heat as he pulled the biscuits out. At least that would give him an excuse for his flushed cheeks.

When he put the hot pan on the counter, Liza handed him a plate. Her gaze was considering.

He could only hope that after last night and this morning, she felt differently about him than she had before.

Because he was still as much in love with her as ever.

NATHAN PUSHED the herd of cattle to the far pasture. Five weeks later, and he still didn't have peace about how he'd left things with Janie.

He reined in his horse as the cattle dispersed from the tight knot of thirty to amble in the pasture, some of them already stopping to graze.

He waved off the neighbor boy he'd hired to help with moving the animals.

He couldn't stop thinking about her.

The way he'd left things with Janie felt... wrong.

He could hardly believe the things the woman on the train platform in Cottonwood Cove had said about her. But hadn't Janie herself hinted at a failed relationship?

He stared at the distant mountains, the sky purpling overhead as the sun sank toward the horizon. He didn't want to go home to his empty house and cook supper. Then sit in his empty parlor until it was time to sleep.

He wanted Janie.

That day spent with her in the boardinghouse... her laughter, her smile.

He couldn't imagine Janie trying to trap someone into marriage. So, what...? Had she been jilted then? That thought made him angry. Almost as angry as imagining her with another man.

He loved her.

He just needed to be sure.

He needed Rob's advice, but the man wasn't here.

But that didn't mean Nathan couldn't seek him out.

Rob accompanied them to the train station.

Liza was glad he'd come. Conscious of his every move, though there'd been no opportunity for them to speak privately this morning.

Janie, dressed but face still flushed with sleep, had wandered into the dining room as Liza and Rob had been setting the table.

The lively conversation had continued during the meal, and Liza had felt at home. Even Rob's puppy gnawing on the toe of her shoe beneath the table had made her happy.

Now he stayed close beside her as they navigated the busy platform, Janie slightly behind them.

Liza felt a stirring of hope. No private words had been exchanged, but Rob had caught and held her gaze several times throughout the morning. Was there a chance he might forget her disastrous refusal of his proposal?

Because after all of this, she wouldn't refuse him again.

Perhaps he would say *something* when they parted ways before she boarded.

She smiled at the ticket agent, but the man appeared frazzled and harried. He handed her the tickets to Calvin and then—

"Wait." The ticket agent pushed a piece of paper across the counter to her.

"What's this?" she asked.

He was already motioning to the person waiting behind her.

She stepped out of line and out of the flow of traffic. Rob was at her elbow.

"What is it?" Janie asked curiously.

"A wire." Liza's eyes ran down to the bottom of the page first. "From Mama."

If she'd heard about the train robbery, Mama's nerves must've been frayed.

But as Liza's eyes tracked across the page, the bottom fell out of her stomach. The wire wasn't about Liza and Janie at all.

Lydia ran away with Wickham. Papa has left to search. No idea where. Lydia is ruined.

No. No, this couldn't be. Not her little sister. In a daze, Liza handed the missive to Janie with shaking hands.

She could barely bring herself to raise her eyes to Rob's face. "It's my sister—"

"No!" Janie's cry drew curious gazes from several nearby passengers.

A loud whistle from the train made Liza jump. It chugged closer to the station, noise growing.

Rob was close, his hand beneath her elbow to steady her.

He wouldn't want to stay close, not after she told him.

Liza licked her lips with a tongue that felt thick and dry. "Lydia has run away with Mr. Wickham." Tears rushed to her eyes even as she said the words, blurring Rob and everything else in her vision.

His hand fell away from her arm, and even without touching him, she felt his sudden tension.

She blinked and wiped at her eyes.

The train whooshed into the station with a squeal of brakes, swirling hot air and dust.

"Maybe they eloped," Janie said hopefully, though tears clogged her voice as well.

Danna and Chas came closer, concerned.

Liza laughed bitterly. "No chance. Lydia's reputation will be ruined forever. *If* she makes it home from God-knows-where."

Janie flinched, looking down. Liza understood her reaction. Janie well knew how words could be like knives when wielded by gossips.

A horrible thought rose. Would they have to leave Calvin? Would rumors swirl around the whole family? Again?

The conductor called for passengers to board.

Liza's feet and limbs felt leaden. She didn't want to get on the train. She didn't want things to end like this between her and Rob. This was... this was even worse than her refusal.

His face was white, his jaw set. His eyes were hooded and dark.

"We must go," Danna said softly. She sent a concerned gaze to Rob. The man was like stone.

Danna and Chas ushered Liza and Janie onto the train.

Liza looked back as they climbed the steps to the train compartment.

Rob hadn't waited. Hadn't said goodbye. He'd already turned to leave and was striding through the crowd, his broad shoulders set.

More tears blurred her vision as she settled into a seat next to Janie.

"This is a disaster," Janie whispered.

It was worse than that.

Rob had warned her about Wickham in his letter. But because of her embarrassment about how things had ended—her foolishness in misjudging him—she hadn't shared any of it with her family.

And now Lydia had fallen victim to Wickham's charms.

Liza could only pray her sister hadn't been compromised, though it was a foolish hope.

For herself, she held out no hope.

She would likely never see Rob again.

23

Rob was awake before dawn the next morning. He'd already dressed and was shoving a change of clothes into his saddlebags at the kitchen table while he gulped his too-hot coffee.

He was a fool.

He hadn't even attempted to comfort Liza at the train station yesterday, though it was clear the telegraph her mother had sent had devastated her.

He'd been stunned by her news, mind already whirling with what he might do to track down Wickham and fix things for Liza.

He'd also been afraid that if he reached out to comfort her, she would reject him again. With her sister looking on. And his.

All that wonderful morning she'd spent under his roof, he'd wanted to ask her to take a walk. Wanted to speak with her privately. Find out if her feelings toward him had changed.

They hadn't had a chance.

She'd spent time with her sister, sitting on his parlor sofa and whispering. Or chatting with Danna, who'd fallen into an easy camaraderie with her.

Each time he'd gotten up the nerve, she'd look away shyly.

Maybe that was his answer.

If her feelings for him had changed, wouldn't she have given him some sign?

He'd stalled out on packing his saddlebag, lost in thoughts of Liza, when Charlie banged in the back door, startling him.

"Your horse is saddled, boss. Sure you don't want me to come with you?"

He doubted it would be his finest hour if and when he came face to face with Wickham. He didn't need Charlie there to witness it.

"I need you here," he said. "To watch over the place." Rob secured the flap and lifted the saddlebag.

Charlie shifted his feet.

"You got something else to say?"

Charlie winced, like maybe he didn't want to say what was on his mind. But they'd been friends for years, so of course he opened his trap. "You sure you want to do this? Ride into the middle of the little gal's family drama?"

He had to. If there was any chance of saving the situation...

"Liza was devastated. If I can help erase that..." He knew she loved her sisters.

Charlie cleared his throat. "And ah... if, after all this, Liza still feels the same as she did before?"

Rob didn't want to think about that. He leveled an even gaze on his foreman. "She shouldn't have to be afraid for her sister. And Lydia needs somebody to find her, to…help her." He couldn't forget the devastation on Katy's face last Christmas. Couldn't forget how hurt and angry Danna had been.

Didn't want that for Liza.

He strode past his foreman and friend and out in to the predawn darkness.

His horse greeted him with a whicker, and Rob secured his saddlebags and checked his saddle cinch out of habit.

He swung up into the saddle, surveying the shadow of his barn in the darkness. Yesterday, it had been so easy to imagine Liza here. To think about coming inside after a long day working the cattle to be greeted by her pretty smile. They'd worked together seamlessly in the kitchen. He'd even made her laugh once, although it had been at his expense.

He loved her.

And whether she would ever return his feelings was a mystery.

But he'd never forgive himself if he didn't try to fix this for her.

DAYS PASSED WITH NO WORD.

With Papa gone, Liza and Janie took over running the store completely.

Liza used it as an escape from Mama's constant vacillating between sobbing hysterically and falling into a restless sleep, still sniffling. In turn, she blamed Lydia for ruining their lives and feared for Lydia's reputation. In Mama's darkest moments, she feared for her daughter's very life.

Liza couldn't find the courage to tell anyone what she knew about Wickham. There was always the chance he'd come to his senses and abandon Lydia unscathed.

It was a wild hope, but it was better than nothing.

With so many hours spent in the store, Liza used the opportunity to put into place what she'd learned working in the Collinses' store.

Boots.

It was as simple as that.

Papa had always insisted on displaying their finest work in the window. Saddles and tooled belts and coin purses. But Collins displayed nothing but boots in all shapes and sizes.

Strategic displays inside the store made it easy to sell items the customer hadn't even realized they needed.

The store had enjoyed more sales this week than it had all of last month, and she'd even filled two special orders for new saddles.

If Lydia had been home, if things had been normal, the increased sales would've been cause for celebration.

With Lydia gone, it felt like too little, too late. Liza had wanted to rescue the family, but her silence had done the opposite.

Would they have to leave Calvin, like they'd left Cottonwood Cove?

She had no answers.

Rob found them in Rock Springs.

He'd spent over a week asking in every hotel, bordello and tavern in every small town in the area. He finally lucked out when a hotel clerk admitted they'd taken a room upstairs.

It'd been late in the evening, so Rob bided his time and took a room himself.

In the morning, he sat in the hotel restaurant with a view toward the stairwell.

Surprisingly, it was Lydia who descended first. She was alone and looked younger than her seventeen years, hair in a simple bun and wisping around her face. He could see Liza in the shape of her jaw and the bridge of her nose, and a fierce sense of protectiveness rose up.

She caught sight of him and hesitated.

He tried to imagine how Danna's charge, the orphan Katy, would respond and made himself smile. He waved her over.

She came after a slight hesitation.

"Mr. Darcy. What are you doing here?" There was definitely suspicion in her voice and narrowed eyes.

He turned the question back on her. "What are you doing here?"

She took a half step back.

And he heard Liza's voice from his memories. *You're high-handed and bossy.*

He'd gone about winning Liza all wrong and messed up completely.

This time, he'd take a different approach. Lydia's future depended on it. And maybe his and Liza's did, too.

He worked to show a smile, something neutral, something that hid his judgmental thoughts. "It's nice to see a friendly face. Join me for breakfast?"

She almost looked as if she would refuse, but her stomach gurgled.

He pointed to the carafe of coffee and the empty china cup on the opposite side of the table.

She sank into the chair and reached for the carafe immediately.

The waitress brought the breakfast plate he'd ordered to the table, her gaze bouncing between him and Lydia.

He picked up the plate and put it on Lydia's side of the table.

Her eyes widened.

"Bring another?" he asked the waitress, who nodded and hurried off.

Lydia scooped up the fork and began shoveling scrambled eggs into her mouth. More than what was polite.

She picked up the biscuit, not even bothering with butter or jam, and stuffed a bite in her mouth. Her eyes closed momentarily as if she were overcome.

Wickham wasn't feeding her properly, that much was clear.

Upon closer inspection, her dress was slightly wrinkled, and tiny lines fanned from her eyes.

"Are you alone?" he asked bluntly.

She shook her head, mouth still too full to speak.

"Where is Wickham?"

Her eyes flashed, and she put down her fork. It clinked against the fancy china plate.

"There's no use pretending," he said. "I know you ran off with him."

She gripped the edge of the table with both hands and started to stand.

He was making a hash of this. Liza's face flashed in his mind, the devastation she'd shown when she'd read her mother's wire.

"Your family is worried about you."

He was sure she'd storm away but, amazingly, she slumped back into the chair, her eyes filling with tears.

He panicked. He hadn't meant to make her cry. Now what?

She picked up her napkin and sniffled noisily into it.

When she looked up at him, all her suspicion was gone. "I… I thought things would be d-different."

He nodded slowly, carefully. She was like a spooked calf. No sudden movements…

She wiped her cheeks with the napkin. "He s-said we'd be married, but he hasn't looked for a preacher. He goes out in the evenings and leaves me alone... and he's gone all night!"

The waitress was heading their way with his plate of steaming food in hand, but when she saw Lydia, her eyes widened and she turned around, disappearing back into the kitchen with his breakfast.

He held back a sigh. His stomach grumbled its displeasure.

He waited for her to calm down.

She blew her nose noisily into the napkin and lifted wet eyes to him.

"Do you want to go home?" he asked. "I can make that happen."

She shrugged miserably. "I think... I might love him. And we've—"

He lifted his hand to stop her. He didn't want to hear details. "Is he upstairs now?"

She nodded.

"Why don't you finish your breakfast." Since it seemed he wouldn't get any. "And I'll go up and talk to him."

She passed him the key to their room, and he moved through the lobby.

He hesitated at the foot of the stairs. He really didn't want to confront Wickham. The man had betrayed him once already, had proved himself a cad.

But Rob wouldn't fail Liza.

Upstairs, Rob unlocked the door to the room. The curtains had been pulled, leaving it dim.

Clothes littered the floor, and it stank of body odor.

Wickham snored softly from the bed.

Rob went straight to the windows and pulled back the curtains, letting bright morning sunlight stream into the room.

"Whaa—?"

Wickham rolled in the bed, but his head remained on the pillow.

Rob went to the bed and yanked off the quilt. Luckily, the man wore long johns.

"What the—?" Wickham sat up in bed, saw Rob and scrabbled backwards toward the headboard.

Rob saw the pistol on the dresser and quickly stepped over to pick it up. He held it loosely at his side.

Wickham was rumpled and tussled, and there was a fading bruise beneath one jaw. His eyes were red-rimmed and wary.

"What do you want?" Wickham demanded.

"I want you to do right by that girl weeping into her napkin downstairs."

Wickham's expression turned hard. "What I do with Lydia is none of your business."

Rob took stock of the man. Wickham was right. His life wasn't any of Rob's business.

But Grandfather had seen something in Wickham of value. What had happened to that young man so full of promise?

Was there a glint of vulnerability behind Wickham's hard exterior?

Wickham had betrayed Rob's trust once. Could he find a way to forgive the other man? For Lydia's sake?

For Liza's?

He breathed in deeply, releasing all the bitterness and anger he'd held toward Wickham with one long exhale.

"Is this what you really want for your life?"

Wickham sneered.

"Spending the night in taverns when you have a girl at home who thinks better of you?"

Something shifted behind Wickham's eyes, and Rob could only pray his words were getting through.

"You've done a great job pulling the wool over her eyes," Rob said. "She thinks you're charming and genuine. She loves you."

Wickham frowned. He stood and reached for a pair of trousers on the floor beside the bed, then quickly pulled them on. "I don't see how our relationship is any of your business."

Rob wouldn't let slip that he cared about Liza. Wickham would turn that knowledge to his advantage.

"She deserves better," Rob pressed.

Wickham threw his hands up. "What are you going to do? Aim that pistol at my back all the way to the parson's house?"

It was a tempting thought.

"Or give me a chunk of money as a wedding gift?"

"No. To both." He took a breath, felt Grandfather there beside him. "I'm going to give you a chance. Like Grandfather wanted. Like Grandfather did."

Wickham stared at him.

"He saw something good in you. Since he's been gone, I haven't seen a trace of it."

Wickham's expression lost its hint of openness and shifted into something ugly.

Rob continued anyway. "But that doesn't mean you can't have a second chance to be the man Grandfather thought you were. The man that the girl downstairs believes you are." He paced to the wardrobe and put the gun on top of it. "I'm willing to give you a reference. I've got a friend in Idaho looking to hire a couple of cowboys with a chance to be foreman eventually."

Wickham stared at him, suspicion clouding his features. "Why? What's in it for you?"

It would make Liza happy. And that was enough.

"I'll do it for Grandfather." He leveled a finger on Wickham. "But you have to marry Lydia. Today. Take her home to her family and prove you've done right by her. Settle their minds."

Wickham shrugged, looking out the window now. Rob could see the wheels in his mind churning.

"Grandfather believed in you," Rob said, hoping to plunge the knife in further. "You can still live up to that."

. . .

Rob stood at the back of the small church as Wickham and Lydia said their vows. The preacher's wife and a young man who might've been the hotel clerk stood up for them.

Lydia was beaming. She wore a new dress—which Rob would never admit to purchasing, though he'd had it sent to their hotel—and carrying a bouquet of wildflowers.

Wickham pulled at his tie once, but he didn't seem as nervous as Rob would've expected. Maybe, just maybe, he'd treat Lydia right. At least while he worked for a friend, Rob could keep tabs on him. Beyond that...

They exchanged simple silver rings, and Lydia beamed again.

Before Rob had left the hotel earlier, he'd convinced Lydia to send a telegraph to her family, to let them know she was coming home for a visit.

He'd also extracted a promise that she wouldn't speak to anyone of his involvement.

The last thing he wanted was for Liza to find out and feel obligated toward him.

And something Charlie'd said as Rob had rushed out of the house that last morning had stuck in his mind, rubbing like a burr beneath the saddle.

What if you do this and she still doesn't want you?

In his head, he'd replayed those last hours with Liza on his ranch. Again and again.

Liza had been softening toward him. He was sure of it. But was it enough?

Her refusal had been adamant, and even though he'd said he cared for her, she'd made no hint of any feelings for him.

Was he a fool, hoping for something out of reach?

24

Hot and dusty and tired, Rob rode onto his ranch three days later. Charlie was there to take his horse.

Rob took off his Stetson as he hit the porch, giving it a good whack against his thigh to loose some of the road dust.

When he stepped in to the kitchen, he stopped short.

"Nate. What're you doing here?"

He accepted a back-slapping hug from his friend.

"It's about time. Charlie let me in. I've been making myself at home for two days." Nathan settled back in at the table as Rob poured himself a glass of cool water and leaned against the counter.

"I had no idea you were coming up this direction," Rob said.

"I needed to talk to you."

Rob let one eyebrow go up. "A letter wouldn't suffice?"

"Not for this matter."

Nathan's hat rested on the tabletop, and he grabbed it, bringing it down to his lap and twirling it between his hands. "It's about Janie."

With all his focus on Lydia and Wickham, Rob hadn't had a spare minute for anything else.

"Is she all right?"

"Of course. As far as I know." Nathan shook his head. "I'd forgotten about the drama with her sister—apparently, she eloped. There's been gossip all over town..." He shook his head, slashing one hand through the air. "None of that matters." He took a deep breath. "I'm in love with Janie. And I think she cares for me too."

Rob couldn't help the smile that twitched at his friend's fervor.

Nathan flicked a look in his direction.

"Good," said Rob.

"What?" Nathan burst out of his seat. "Two months ago you told me she was indifferent."

Rob shrugged. "I was wrong."

It was easier to make the admission than he'd thought.

Nathan narrowed his eyes, his suspicion so out of character that Rob had to stifle a smile. "What aren't you telling me?"

So very much.

"After Hildy, I knew you second-guessed yourself. You aren't the kind of person who likes to think the worst of others, so I told myself it was my duty to protect you. Like an older brother might."

Nathan smiled wryly at that. At least he hadn't thrown a punch, like a younger brother might.

"I mistook Janie's shy nature for indifference. I was wrong."

Nathan wore such a look of relief, Rob clapped him on the shoulder. Nathan would make it right. He could charm himself back into Janie's good graces.

And he hadn't asked how Rob knew. That was a relief. Rob wasn't ready to confess his interactions with Liza just yet.

But then Nathan turned serious again. "That's not all of it."

Nathan told a long story, something about getting sick on a train. Janie'd rescued him, but they'd had to lie, say they were married, to secure a room.

Then the story turned dark. Nathan had been accosted by a woman on the train platform who'd made terrible accusations against Janie.

Liza had hinted, but Rob hadn't expected *this*.

"That is concerning," Rob said. "Has Janie spread any gossip about the nights you spent together in Cottonwood Cove?"

"Not a peep. I've gone past hoping her father might show up at my door with a shotgun."

Rob grinned, then became serious again.

"Did you believe the accusations against Janie?"

Nathan frowned. "I am not as good at reading people as you are. But I can't even… Janie's so innocent, so… I cannot imagine her having done what that woman said."

In this case, Rob thought Nathan's assessment spot on.

"But why would someone lie about Janie like that, if there wasn't some truth to it?" Nathan threw out the question, then slumped in his chair.

Rob shrugged. "Perhaps her son intended to compromise Janie but was interrupted. He could've easily lied to his mother to place the blame on her."

And Janie was innocent enough, she would've been caught in the middle.

Nathan's eyes flashed. He stood suddenly, snatched his hat a moment before it slid from his lap to the floor. "Maybe I should go back and ask the man myself."

Rob laughed aloud, unused to seeing his easygoing friend so riled up.

"Or," Rob suggested, fighting a smile, "perhaps you return home and win the girl, and then you could stop by later to thank him."

Nathan smiled. "There is that." He sat back down. "Do you think she'll forgive me?"

"For being an idiot?"

"For having doubts. I was too shocked at the time to ask her about it. Now it's been weeks. We haven't spoken."

"I think if you tell her about Hildy, she'll understand."

Nathan pulled a face. "I should admit to being a fool?"

"With much groveling," Rob suggested.

Nathan smiled slightly. "Hildy seems so long ago. I can never thank you enough for rescuing me from that relationship."

"It will be thanks enough if you patch things up with Janie."

Nathan tossed his hat back on the table and leaned forward. "You'll help me devise a plan to win her back?"

"Of course."

It was the least he could do for ruining things in the first place.

THE MOMENT THE TELEGRAPH ARRIVED, it was as if a switch had been flipped inside Mama.

Lydia was married.

Mama beamed with pride and pleasure. She sometimes fell into silence, staring at nothing, a bemused smile on her face.

Janie and Kitty whispered together often, speculating how it had happened.

It was as if they'd all forgotten that Lydia had run off with Wickham, would've ruined herself if they hadn't married.

For days, gossip had swirled around Calvin. Hopefully, Lydia's arrival this afternoon on Wickham's arm would quell the rumors.

Liza could only hope that her sister would be happy. If he

remained the scoundrel he'd started out as, Lydia would suffer a miserable marriage. Liza could only pray he'd change.

She pled a headache and begged off meeting the train at the station.

She was setting the table for supper when she heard the distant train whistle.

It made her think of Rob.

Things had ended so suddenly on the train platform in Sheridan. She'd hoped for some sign from him that he still had feelings for her. Then the telegraph had interrupted. And above her own fears, she'd felt Rob withdraw at the mention of Wickham.

Wickham, who was a part of their family now. If ever there was a reason for Rob to avoid her, here it was. He hated Wickham.

She might hate him too. Especially if he didn't treat Lydia right.

She dawdled over the place settings until noise from the boardwalk carried up through the small front window of their apartment. She'd know Mama's pealing laugh anywhere.

Janie came through the door first and went immediately to the wash basin. While she rinsed her dusty hands, she peered over her shoulder at Liza. "Are you sure you're all right? I know there was... something between you and Wickham."

That first day of flirtation seemed so long ago now.

"It's not that—"

The others came through the door, cutting her off.

Lydia, Mama, and Kitty were embroiled in a loud, chatty conversation. Wickham and Papa came in behind, and Liza couldn't help it when Wickham's gaze met hers.

Without her permission, a hot flush rose in her face. She jerked her eyes away.

She didn't lie to herself. Any feelings she might've tendered for the man had been destroyed the moment she'd read Rob's letter.

But there was also a part of her that didn't want her family to find out about his past—or that Liza knew about it.

Supper was full of lively conversation interspersed with Lydia showing off the thin silver band as often as she could.

After supper, Liza and Janie washed up, content to listen as the women continued their chat. Wickham sat next to Papa in the corner, looking conspicuously out of place. Papa had a newspaper open and seemed to ignore everyone else.

"And then Mr. Darcy—"

Liza dropped the plate she'd been scrubbing into the water with a *ploop*. Hot water splashed on her dress, but she barely felt it.

"Rob was there?" She turned. Her voice had been louder than she'd intended. Rob had been involved in the fiasco with Lydia?

Lydia shot her a quelling look. "I know he insulted your pride before, but he's not a monster."

If only she knew.

"I promised I wouldn't tell but... he accidentally bumped into us at our hotel and said he wanted to talk to Wickham, and the next thing I knew, we were at the altar."

Oh, Lydia. No doubt Rob had engineered the whole thing.

Why, though? No matter how she turned the matter over in her head, she couldn't fathom a reason for Rob's actions.

25

Two days after Lydia and Wickham's departure to their new home in Idaho, Janie stood before the tiny looking glass in her shared bedroom. Liza and Kitty had already gone, joining Mama and Papa at the shop downstairs. The Founders' Day town-wide picnic was upon them, and Janie wished she didn't have to go.

With Lydia gone, it seemed quieter at home and around the shop. Janie felt... restless. Liza's change to the displays had brought in more foot traffic, and though the store was busier and more profitable, it felt as if there were something missing.

Or maybe that was simply because Nathan was missing from her life.

It shouldn't have mattered. Theirs had been a whirlwind courtship. Perhaps friendship was the better word. But she'd fallen for him deeply, and his absence was painful.

Everyone in town would be at the picnic today.

And everyone would see Nathan avoid her.

Everything will be forgotten, she told herself.

It had been over a month since she'd seen him last. With the time spent with Auntie M and then those couple days spent on Rob's ranch, he should be out of her thoughts. Forgotten.

He wasn't.

She missed him. Longed to see him again, though it would be painful after his silence on their train ride from Cottonwood Cove to Calvin.

She'd spent enough time in front of the looking glass, adjusting the elaborate braid around the crown of her head, even weaving a ribbon into it. She forced herself to go downstairs. Join her family.

Two steps out into the Wyoming wind, and all her primping was all for naught.

She stifled a sigh as she followed the family down Main Street to the field behind the schoolhouse, where they joined the other townspeople in a display of colorful blankets, all spread out.

Groups chatted in clusters. She shielded her eyes with one hand and scanned the area, loosing a sigh of relief when she didn't spot Nathan.

It must be relief she felt, not disappointment.

She waved hello to Merritt and Danna and Chas but was content to remain on the blanket with Liza while Mama and Kitty flitted around, chatting and giggling.

And then a tall shadow fell over the picnic blanket.

A roasted chicken balanced in both hands, Janie looked up, sure her mouth had fallen open slightly because there stood—

"Mr. Bingley!" Mama cried. She and Kitty must've been close, because they now stood at the corner of the blanket.

"How have you been?" Liza asked warmly when the silence went on for a beat too long.

Janie felt heat slip up her neck and into her face. She looked down, curls from her ruined hairstyle slipping across her cheek in the brisk wind.

Liza took the chicken from her shaking hands, and Janie hid them in the folds of her apron.

Hussy. Seductress. Edna's names from the train platform echoed in her memories, and she so desperately wanted to run and hide. But there was no place to go.

Nathan cleared his throat, but before he could say anything, Mama interrupted.

"I'd heard you were out of town. I hope your trip went well? To St. Louis, I mean."

Unbidden, Janie's gaze jumped to meet his. She would never forget being in Cottonwood Cove with him, cocooned in their own space for those precious hours.

One corner of his mouth tipped as if he might be thinking about that time too. "It was unremarkable."

"Now that you're back in town," Mama said, "you simply *must* come for supper sometime. If you tell me your favorites, I'm sure Janie and I could make a meal you'd simply love."

Janie's face flushed hotter. Why must Mama always behave like this?

Red had crept into Nathan's cheeks as well. "Certainly. In fact, if you wouldn't mind terribly, I'd like to steal Janie away for a short—"

"Girls! Oh, hello, Mr. Bingley." Wanda and Violet, two friends of Liza's, stumbled onto the edge of their circle.

"Janie and Liza, you promised to help with the planting for today. You can't back out now."

Violet giggled. "Mr. Bingley, you can join us, if you'd like."

She'd completely forgotten about the project she'd agreed to assist with. Several young women in town had formed the Calvin Beautification Committee, and one of this summer's projects included filling planters all along Main Street with seedlings.

Janie stood, brushing away a wrinkle in her skirt. Her heart was pounding. Why did Nathan want to walk with her?

And surely he'd leave now that she was committed to the ridiculous activity.

But he didn't walk away. "I'd love to."

Oh, why had she ever agreed to help with the project?

As they passed through the crowd and walked back toward Main Street, Liza sent a wide-eyed look over her shoulder when Nathan couldn't see. Janie's stomach jumped like a whole passel of grasshoppers.

Liza threaded her arms through the other two young women's elbows and ushered them onto the boardwalk first, leaving Janie to walk at Nathan's side.

They reached the boardwalk, and he extended his hand to her.

He was only being polite, she told herself. But it didn't stop her pulse from thundering in her temples.

And then he didn't let go. He clasped her hand, allowing them to remain linked.

"Hi, Mr. Bingley!" Schoolmarm Merritt Harding called out.

He waved. With his other hand.

Janie's face burned.

Even when they joined the group in front of the general store, he didn't let go of her.

Not until someone pushed a crate of seedlings toward them and he was forced to relinquish her hand to take it. She accepted a small trowel and watering can.

They had to complete two planters and were assigned those in front of the Calvin Bank and Trust, which stood toward the far end of the dusty Main Street.

Surely it couldn't take that long to weed out two containers and plant the flats of seedlings they'd been assigned.

Then she could escape from Nathan's presence and go back to the picnic.

NATHAN'S HEART pounded as Janie settled her skirts around her legs and kneeled on the dusty street.

Rob's encouragement had gone a long way in convincing him that he wanted to ask Janie to marry him. Immediately. He didn't want to waste any more time without her by his side.

But when he'd ridden into town, he'd seen the picnic being set up and remembered the town event. It had completely slipped his mind in his quest for Janie's hand.

And then her mother. Her mother! He couldn’t get a word in edgewise.

This was better, even if they were surrounded by chatting women. They were semi-alone, and all he had to do was pluck up the courage to say what he needed to say.

Except she didn't look at him as she plunged her fingers into the rich, brown dirt, plucking out several weeds with ruthless abandon and tossing them in the street. Was she angry that he'd all but abandoned her after she'd cared for him in Cottonwood Cove?

Was she hurt?

She had every right to feel both. He'd bungled things terribly. He could only hope they could be repaired.

He wasn't good at this. Didn't know how to open the conversation.

He swallowed hard. "How've you been? Rob told me about the train robbery. That must've been frightening."

And if he could, he'd prevent anything like that from happening to her ever again.

She winced slightly. He wouldn't have noticed if he hadn't been watching her so closely.

"I'm fine." She tossed another weed out to the side. She still didn't look at him, her focus on the planter.

He took the trowel and used it to measure out a dozen spots for the seedlings. She glanced at him sideways.

He dug the first hole as she reached into the crate for the first seedling. She cupped the dirt surrounding its roots in both hands and placed it in the small hole he'd made.

He moved to capture her hand, but she jerked it back quickly.

A glance at her face revealed nothing. Her eyes were focused down, her lashes hiding any glimpse of her emotion.

Maybe she hadn't guessed his intention. Or maybe she was embarrassed because they were both covered with dirt.

He cleared his throat and tried again. "I've had a letter from Mindy. She seems to have settled in all right. She's taken a job with a seamstress. I think she's hoping to meet someone..."

And now he was rambling.

Why wouldn't she give him some kind of sign? In Cottonwood Cove, he'd been certain she held some affection for him, until those moments on the train platform.

Had he crushed the blossom of her affection forever?

He stared at her, falling behind on his hole-digging duties as she planted the next two seedlings.

And a flash of memory brought with it the look in her eyes on the platform. The heartbreaking hurt he'd been given only a glimpse of.

He'd been a part of that, and he would make it right.

He'd opened his mouth to blurt everything he felt when a shadow fell over them both.

"Brought some muslin," Violet said. He'd met her at the barn-raising.

Her arms were full of the stuff. Her grin encompassed them both, though Janie didn't look up to see it. "The Beautification

Committee thought it would look nice draped across the planters."

He shrugged helplessly but Janie nodded. Violet moved off and Janie stood up. For one wild moment, he thought she was leaving. She stepped a couple of feet away and settled in front of the second planter.

While his mind had been spinning, Janie had finished planting the seedlings.

Now she was tearing weeds out of the second planter with a vengeance.

He didn't intend to hurt her more. Didn't want to leave things unfinished between them for a moment longer.

He crouched at her side. "Could we go somewhere and talk?" It's what he'd wanted in the first place.

She shook her head slightly. "I don't think that's a good idea."

He glanced around them. Other folks were working on their own planters, and Wanda and Violet had wandered to the opposite end of the street. No one seemed to be paying them any attention.

So he grabbed Janie's grubby hand in his.

He'd thought she might jerk away, but she froze instead. Finally, finally, she lifted her gaze so he could see her beautiful face.

"I've been a fool." He spoke the words in a low voice, but it didn't detract from his intensity. "I should never have let doubts fester, for you've been nothing but kindness and light in my world. Can you ever forgive me for my silence these past weeks?"

Her eyes had gone round and now filled with tears, though she blinked rapidly.

"I don't—"

"I've been in love with you from the beginning." His heart

thrummed, and he didn't want to hear her refusal. He rushed on. "Probably from the moment you coughed water all over my boots after nearly drowning in the creek. Maybe even from our first dance the night we met."

One tear rolled down her cheek, and he reached for it without thinking, rubbing it away with his thumb. And since his hand was covered in dirt, he left a tiny streak of mud down her cheek.

"Oh dear." He wrinkled his nose and reached into his pocket for his handkerchief, but of course it was streaked with dirt by the time he managed to free it.

She laughed wetly and took it from his fingers anyway, wiping her face quickly.

She wasn't looking away from him now. She was smiling, shining with joy from within.

And his heart started pounding a hopeful rhythm.

"It's the same for me," she whispered, looking up at him with a shy glance. "I fell for you when you carried me so carefully back to your house."

He reached for her hand, and this time she met him halfway.

"I can explain about... about Albert." Her eyes dropped, a flush spreading across her cheeks.

He squeezed her hand. "You don't have to. Whatever lies he and his mother fabricated can't touch you now. I won't let them."

Her gaze came up to meet his again, and they were filled with such hope—her hope gave him wings.

"Would you consider marrying me, if I promised never to be such a fool again?"

Her lips twitched. "Are you sure you could make such a promise?"

"Probably not. I hope to always make a fool of myself over you."

"I think I'd like that very much," she whispered.

"Yeah?" Now his eyes were the ones that were filling with moisture.

She nodded, biting her lower lip.

Joy suffused him, filling up every crevice and crack in his heart. Janie loved him back. And she was going to marry him.

"Soon?" he asked.

"Soon," she promised.

JANIE WAS RADIANT with joy even as the sun set and they settled in to the apartment.

Even Mama's clucking and fluttering didn't seem to faze her, and Liza couldn't help but smile at her sister's effervescent happiness.

Janie would marry Nathan after Sunday services in two weeks. They'd begged off from the picnic and gone on a long walk, Janie wind-blown and well-kissed when they'd returned, judging by the roses in her cheeks.

Now as Liza and Janie settled in for bed, Janie whispered plans for her dress, things she needed to add to her hope chest, and wishes for Liza to find the same happiness she had.

Liza was unbearably happy for her sister, she truly was.

But she couldn't contain the tug of jealousy that pulled at her.

Janie had found her happiness.

And Liza was still alone.

After two weeks, the hope that she'd held onto—that Rob would write or even come for her—had begun to wither.

All she could think of were the words he'd written in his letter. *I will not repeat my proposal.*

26

"Charlotte!"

Liza circled the counter to greet her friend as the woman slipped inside the store, baby in her arms.

Through the window, she could see Mr. Collins and Papa on the boardwalk looking into the store window and gesticulating animatedly.

"What are you doing here?" Liza asked as she embraced her friend. "And look at you!" She cooed to the baby.

"I think William had a bit of cabin fever after playing my nursemaid those weeks. For days, he's been talking about nothing but visiting your father to check on the store."

"How kind." But the bottom of Liza's stomach dropped away. Sales had increased since the changes she'd made. Noticeably. Would Mr. Collins make an offer? There'd been talk when he'd visited the first time.

Would Papa take it?

"I can't believe how big she's grown in such a short time." Liza touched the baby's pudgy hand with one finger.

The door opened and Papa stuck his head through. "Liza, could you join us? There'll be time for visiting later."

Charlotte raised her brows and smiled, waving her hand to shoo Liza on.

The men were staring at the line of children's boots Liza had carefully arranged across the front of the window display.

"How did you come up with this idea?" Mr. Collins asked.

Liza flushed. Was he angry that she'd duplicated what he'd done in his Sheridan store?

"It's ingenious," Mr. Collins went on. "I've always used men's boots to entice people to come in off the street, but you probably get a steady stream of young mothers in, don't you?"

She nodded.

Papa's chest puffed out with pride. "And they usually leave with a belt or a bag for marbles, too."

Mr. Collins gave her an appreciative look.

"What are your numbers since Liza returned from Sheridan?" Mr. Collins asked.

Papa looked to her, and Liza fidgeted. He raised one brow. "Don't act as if you don't have them memorized," he said.

She told them, and Mr. Collins looked even more impressed.

"I want to see the inside." Mr. Collins ducked through the door, where Charlotte pointed to something on the shelves above the counter.

Papa put his arm around Liza's shoulder as they watched from the boardwalk.

"Will he make you an offer?" she asked quietly, heart in her throat.

"I don't know."

"If he does, will you take it?"

Papa looked down on her. "Of all my girls, you've always had the best head for business." He tapped her on the nose. "But it isn't your worry."

After the disaster with Lydia, Liza had realized just how

fragile a reputation could be. Had it really been her fault that Janie had been shamed? Or Edna's for spreading rumors? And Albert's, for not standing up for Janie?

She'd gathered all her courage and spoken to Papa, who'd been shocked to learn that she blamed herself for what had happened. He'd assured her that she was the only one who blamed her and that the responsibility for the family fell on his shoulders. Not hers.

And although it had been hard to let go, she'd finally gained a measure of peace about the mess in Cottonwood Cove. It helped that Janie was deliriously happy with Nathan.

Now Papa squeezed her shoulders. "Thank you for what you've done for the store—for our family."

It was the first time he'd ever said so much, and warmth suffused her. "I love you, Papa."

He squeezed her again. "With Lydia married off and Janie to marry Mr. Bingley, it will take less earnings from the store to support our family. Which means you might consider getting married yourself. There's no one who's caught your fancy?"

She laughed a little desperately, thinking of Rob and how her assumptions had ruined everything. "Papa—"

A shrill voice ringing down the boardwalk interrupted her.

"You! You little conniving—"

Liza whirled to see Maisey striding toward her. What in the world? She glanced over her shoulder, but there was nobody behind save a few folks outside the general store, which was several blocks away.

Was Maisey talking about *her*? *Conniving*?

What?

"Excuse me—" Papa started.

Maisey didn't even take a breath. "Tell me it's not true."

Liza knew her confusion must be etched on her face. "What's not true?"

"I heard a rumor that you've become engaged to Rob Darcy, and I know it's an outright lie."

The words were a blow directly to Liza's middle. She felt as if she couldn't breathe. If she hadn't been so stupid, she could've been married to Rob by now.

"I know you started the gossip—"

"I have never heard anything about it!" Liza cried.

"Rob is supposed to marry my Priscilla."

Liza flinched, only hoping after the fact that neither Papa or Maisey noticed.

"I heard the disturbing rumor and came to hear you confess that you'd spread it—"

"I did no such thing," Liza said. "And surely you traveling all this distance to confront me has exacerbated the rumors, not quelled them." Had the woman traveled all this way just to confront Liza? Why would she do that?

Maisey's face went purple.

"I don't know who you are, but I don't like your accusations against my daughter," Papa said.

Liza felt bolstered by his statement. When Edna had leveled her accusations again Janie, Papa had been silent.

"Your daughter is a conniving—"

"Stop!" Liza said. A woman had come outside and stood on the boardwalk, staring at them. The folks who'd been at the general store had wandered closer, no doubt curious to find out the newest gossip about the Bennett family.

Papa and Maisey both turned surprised glances on Liza at her outburst.

"I am not engaged to Rob," she said. The words cut her throat like glass.

Maisey inhaled deeply, smug satisfaction crossing her expression. "And will you promise to refuse him if he asks?"

Liza inhaled fire, lungs aching and full of smoke and brimstone. Not at the woman's audacious demand, but at what she'd lost. "I won't. And I think you've insulted me enough. Good day."

She turned to retreat inside the store, only then realizing that Mr. Collins and Charlotte stood in the store doorway, wide-eyed.

"Excuse me." She brushed past them and darted to the back stairs.

She slammed into the apartment. Inside, Mama and Janie looked up from their sewing project—something for her wedding gown, no doubt.

Janie put down her needle and fabric immediately. "What's the matter?"

"Nothing." Liza rushed for her bedroom.

"Liza..." came Mama's voice behind her.

"Leave me alone!" she shouted, slamming the bedroom door behind her.

And then when she couldn't hold them back any longer, she dissolved into tears.

She wasn't engaged to Rob, and she never would be.

"...AND then Maisey called Liza a conniving something. I was too far away to hear all of it."

Rob wasn't one to abide gossip. But the mention of Liza's name brought his head around in the small church, cutting off the conversation he'd been having with Charlie as they'd walked toward the exit.

He'd missed three Sunday services in a row thanks to a bunch of growing calves and the branding his herd had demanded. They'd pushed the last of the cattle to be sold to the Sheridan train station just yesterday. Even with a good night's rest, he was exhausted.

And desperate for any news of Liza.

Had the speaker been talking about *his* Liza? Charlie waited in the doorway to the sanctuary, but Rob ignored his foreman for the time being.

He glanced at the woman who'd spoken. Charlotte Collins, the woman whom Liza had come to Sheridan to help.

Rob waved Charlie off and sat on the empty pew near them, hoping to overhear more. The Sunday service had wrapped up nearly a quarter hour ago, but several families still stood inside the little church building, conversing with neighbors and friends. Spring was a busy season for the farmers and ranchers, and they had to take every opportunity for human conversation instead of bovine.

"I was shocked to see her in Calvin at all," Charlotte went on.

Maisey had gone to Calvin? To what purpose?

"She said she'd heard some rumor that Liza was engaged to Rob—"

His heart leapt.

"—but of course Liza denied it."

And fell again.

He'd seen Nathan only four days ago and expected a letter any day announcing Nathan's happy news. He was confident his friend had been able to win Janie back, and he wanted an invite to the wedding.

"*I* have an idea that Priscilla started the rumor, if there even was one. You know she's tired of her mother's meddling..."

If he could get close enough to speak to Charlotte, he could discover a clue as to whether Liza's feelings for him had changed. But he didn't move. He'd never been one for eavesdropping, and doing so now made him feel like a lovesick school boy. Maybe he could pass Charlotte a note when the teacher wasn't looking.

He knew he was a fool, but the knowledge didn't get his rump off the pew.

"And then Maisey demanded Liza say she'd say no if Rob ever asked for her hand" Charlotte's voice dropped—"*and Liza refused*."

At this, he stood, whirling and clutching the back of the pew behind him. Stunned.

Charlotte caught sight of him and flushed, lowering her eyes as if she hadn't just been gossiping about the woman he loved.

If Charlotte's gossip was to be believed, Liza wouldn't refuse him if he proposed again.

Pulse thudding in his temples, he mashed his hat on his head and tipped it to Charlotte. He couldn't help grinning.

Her eyes widened, and no doubt he'd just given her something else to gossip about.

He didn't care.

He had to get to Calvin.

To Liza.

To find out for himself.

27

That same Sunday evening, two days after Maisey's scene on the boardwalk, Liza set the table while Janie checked on her pie for the fifth time.

William and Charlotte had only stayed for a single day, Charlotte anxious to get the baby back home.

Liza hadn't slept well, her mind whirling with thoughts of Maisey and her accusations and whether Rob wanted to marry Priscilla after all.

Probably Priscilla wouldn't reject his suit.

Mama and Janie had tiptoed around her, but now both were distracted by Nathan coming to supper.

The train whistle blew, muted from the edge of town, as Liza dusted behind the counter, and she closed her eyes against an onslaught of pain and memories.

Janie flitted around, adjusting the cushions on their tiny sofa and then leaning over Liza's shoulder to check on the roast she'd pulled from the oven. The pie cooled on a rack on the counter.

When the knock came and Janie opened the door, a tall figure stood behind Nathan on the landing.

Rob.

He'd swept his hat off, and his hair was rumpled and a little crazy. What looked like his Sunday suit was wrinkled, and one lapel was askew.

Her stomach swooped. She nearly dropped the dish but managed to push it onto the stovetop with shaking hands. She clutched the towel between her hands.

He watched her over Nathan's shoulder, his eyes burning with an intensity she didn't know how to read.

Nathan brushed a kiss across Janie's cheek. "I hope you don't mind another guest at the table. I ran into this cowpoke on the boardwalk. He'd just arrived on the evening train." The men exchanged a glance.

And of course Janie was a consummate hostess. "What a lovely surprise. Come in, both of you."

"I hear congratulations are in order," Rob said. His smile for Janie was genuine and held no hint of the doubts he'd expressed to Liza so long ago.

Liza turned her back on them for only a moment, attempting to compose herself.

Her heart was racing with hope and love, and there Rob was, standing with Janie and Nathan, making small talk.

Voices on the landing preceded Mama and Papa and Kitty, who were arriving from an afternoon visit to friends across town.

Liza pasted on a smile as she carried the roast and vegetables to the table.

With Lydia gone, their dinner table had felt larger. Now, with Nathan and Rob joining them, the entire room felt as if it had shrunk like a piece of tanned leather.

Liza ended up across the table and one seat over from Rob, who sat between Papa and Nathan. Papa struck up a lengthy conversation with Rob about his land and the family's heritage in Sheridan County.

Janie was careful to include Liza in conversation, but she couldn't have said later what they'd talked about.

She felt too anxious to choke down much food and had no idea what it tasted like.

She was aware of every glance Rob sent her way. The pointed intensity of his gaze never wavered, though he held his own in conversation with Papa and even teased Nathan several times.

And as Janie rose to fetch the cherry pie she'd spent an hour getting just right, Rob leaned back in his chair, hands clasped over his midsection.

And something touched her foot beneath the table. His boot?

Pulse pounding in her temples, she dared glance across the table at him.

"...had twins," he was saying to Papa. "I've got my foreman bottle-feeding one of them because the mama rejected it."

The man wasn't even looking at her.

But was that tiny smile playing at the corners of his mouth for her benefit? Or for Papa's?

His boot slid along the side of hers, a slight pressure that told her the touch wasn't coincidence after all.

And her heart continued to hammer.

The pie was eaten, though Liza mostly used her fork to push hers around on her plate.

And then the men were standing. Rob was leaving.

"Take a stroll with me?" Nathan asked Janie.

She nodded.

And Nathan turned a friendly gaze on Liza. "Come with us, Liza. You can keep Rob company."

"You don't have to go with him if you don't want to," Mama

muttered behind Liza's back as she carted two plates to the sink.

Liza's face burned.

Something passed between the men again, a glance.

Liza didn't care. She rose from the table trying to steady her wobbly knees. "I'll get my shawl."

ROB TOUCHED the small of Liza's back as their boots hit the bottom step before the boardwalk.

He'd felt a strange mix of anticipation and urgency sitting in her family's apartment. Sort of like the feeling he'd had getting ready to get on a bull for the first—and only—time at a cowboy competition.

He wasn't unaware of the covert glances and appreciative, shy sparkle in Liza's eyes. That, plus what he'd overheard this morning, had his hope flying as high as a boy's kite.

It was pure luck he'd run into Nathan as he'd been making tracks from the train station to Liza's home. It had only taken a few sentences to get Nathan on board with wrangling an invitation for him to supper and a request to walk out with the two women.

That her mother disliked him was obvious, but he couldn't find it in him to care.

He was with Liza.

And she wouldn't say no to his proposal.

Hopefully.

If he didn't muck it up again.

"Would you…?" He extended his elbow, and a wave of relief and warmth rushed through him when her small hand slipped in and rested in the crook of his arm.

They wandered down Main Street as evening fell, the sun streaking the sky with orange and scarlet hues. The boardwalks were empty, all the businesses closed for the evening. Even the saloons at the end of the thoroughfare. He allowed Nathan and Janie to outpace them. He didn't particularly want an audience for what he had to say.

"I'm sorry," he said, then fumbled his words. "I meant to come sooner, but with the end of spring calving and then branding and the cattle sale..."

Her head tilted, and she slanted a glance at him. "As I understand it, you've been busy tracking down my little sister and helping her wedding along."

He grimaced. "I should've known she wouldn't be able to keep a secret."

Liza grinned. "Yes, you should've." She paused. "Thank you."

He frowned. "It was what she wanted, but I hope it wasn't a mistake."

"And thank you for whatever you said to Nathan that inspired him to propose."

He shook his head. "That was mostly Nathan. He's a fool over her."

"My mother is delighted by both events."

He chose not to respond to that.

Liza slanted another glance at him. "I'm sorry she wasn't very welcoming tonight."

He'd have sat on a fire ant hill in the hot summer sun if it meant Liza would smile at him the way she had at supper.

"I overheard something interesting after church services this morning," he murmured. "Mrs. Collins was telling a story about Maisey. And you."

She colored, averting her eyes. Finally, she said, "Yes, she was here."

His heart was racing, but he couldn't quit now. Nathan and Janie were far enough ahead, and they didn't notice when he stopped and turned to face Liza. He took both her hands in his.

"I'm sorry if she was unkind to you, but what Mrs. Collins said has given me the deepest hope." He inhaled deeply. "If your feelings for me remain what they were in May, stop me now. I won't say another word."

He let the pause linger between them, was gratified when she only gazed up at him with shining eyes.

He let go of her hands to clasp her waist gently. "My love for you is even stronger now than it was then. I still want to marry you, if you'll have me. Brownie misses you. I miss your smile at all hours of the day. I can't promise that I'll always know the right way to woo you or the perfect words to say, but my love for you will never fail."

Her smile turned tremulous, and she took a deep breath. "How could I refuse a proposal like that?"

Joy thrilled through him, and he lowered his head to take her lips in a sweet kiss. Emotion wracked him, and he broke off the kiss but hugged her close.

Her hands went behind his neck, and she threaded her fingers into the hair at his nape, sending fire down his back straight to his gut.

"I've regretted my response to your first proposal every day," she whispered. "Can you forgive me for my callousness?"

He squeezed her waist. "I could've handled things better."

Her chin moved against his shoulder. "You'll have to speak to my father."

Anticipation and dread mixed again. She was worth the trouble.

"Janie and Nathan are getting married two weeks from today," she said. "Perhaps we should make it a double wedding?"

He grinned. "Done."

EPILOGUE

"Mama will be upset about the rain," Janie said softly.

They were the only two in their bedroom, so there was no worry of being overheard. They'd rushed home after the Sunday morning service to don the dresses Mama had splurged on. Rob and Nathan waited at the church with their wedding guests.

Liza caught Janie's eye in the looking glass as she checked that her hair hadn't come out of the braided bun Janie had so carefully designed and grinned.

"Will you miss Mama fussing over you?" Liza asked.

Janie considered the question, her head tilting slightly. "Maybe a little."

Mama's hovering had been even more persistent in the two weeks before the double wedding. Rob had stayed overnight with Nathan that first night but then had to return to Sheridan. He'd arrived on yesterday's train and spent all afternoon with the Bennetts.

Liza had apologized to Rob on more than one occasion, like

when Mama had attempted to make a four-course meal, most of which had been inedible.

Rob had borne it with a patient smile, and when she'd brought it up again on a private walk, he'd kissed her to distraction and reminded her she'd be far away from Mama soon enough.

Janie's lips quivered slightly. "I can't believe you'll be in Sheridan."

Liza turned to her sister, reaching for her hand. "It's not so far. We'll come down for Christmas. Maybe sooner."

Janie sniffled. "And Nathan and I can come to you."

"See? It'll be fine. Besides, Nathan is so besotted with you that he won't allow you time to be lonely for me."

Janie giggled. "I never knew it was possible to be this happy."

"Shall we return to the church before the men wonder if we've changed our minds?"

Janie nodded. "Let me check your skirt once more."

Liza whirled, the pale blue fabric she'd chosen for her wedding gown floating around her.

"It's perfect," Janie said.

"Now you."

Janie turned, the pale pink gingham hugging her slender curves in all the right places, the skirt flaring around her ankles.

"You're beautiful," Liza said.

Janie clutched her hands. "Promise you'll write once a week."

Liza laughed. "I'm not sure I'll have that much news to share. I expect Rob won't make me cross *quite* that often."

He'd felt badly about the ranch calling him away in light of their engagement and had returned with a stack of letters hand-delivered. She'd only had time to read two before exhaustion had overcome her last night. She couldn't wait to read his words of love in the rest.

She pulled Janie through the bedroom door, where Papa and Mama and Kitty waited to walk with them to the church.

Mama dissolved into tears the moment she spied Janie.

It was Papa's hug for Liza that almost sent her into her own spate of tears as he gave a wet sniffle. "I'll miss you, Liza dear."

"I'll miss you too, Papa."

But her heart tripped with excitement as they pressed out the apartment door and outside.

"MRS. BENNETT WILL COMPLAIN about the weather all afternoon," Nathan murmured.

Rob considered his friend. "Do you mind very much?"

Nathan grinned. "Nothing can ruin this day for me."

They stood together near the front of the tiny Calvin church, waiting for Janie and Liza.

A small crowd of friends and the preacher had remained in the sanctuary after the morning service. They spoke in low voices, leaving Rob and Nathan to their own devices.

Danna and Chas sat on the front row with their toddler daughter and their adopted daughter, Katy. Danna was beaming. When he'd broken the news of his engagement, she'd confessed to her suspicions all along. His sister, the detective.

Janie appeared first in the open double doors, and Rob heard Nathan's quick intake of air.

For certain, Janie was lovely, but it was Liza's appearance on her father's other arm that put a catch in his own breathing.

Liza was beautiful. He'd seen her during the worship service, but she looked different now. It wasn't just the dress, either. It was the love shining in her eyes that seemed brighter than ever. He hoped seeing her never got old. That he never forgot the feeling—the outright joy that suffused him right now.

She smiled, her gaze never leaving his. Her eyes were shining, like she might be close to tears.

For so many weeks, this moment had seemed out of reach. His every dream was coming true. He was marrying Liza.

The trio reached the end of the carpeted floor runner, and Mr. Bennett handed off both girls.

Rob took Liza's hands in his, peripherally aware of Nathan and Janie linking hands as well.

"You look beautiful," he whispered.

Soft pink rose in her face. "You already told me," she whispered back. "This morning."

"I'll probably tell you again before the day is over."

Her eyes sparkled up at him.

The preacher started talking, and Rob clasped her hands, content to hold her as the man talked about God's love and the institution of marriage. And then it was time to exchange vows.

Nathan was first. Rob heard the catch in his friend's voice as he promised his life to Janie.

And then it was Rob's turn.

His voice was rough with emotion as he repeated after the preacher. "I take thee, Liza, to be my wedded wife, to have and to hold from this day forward, for better for worse, for richer for poorer, in sickness and in health, to love and to cherish, till death us do part."

Her eyes sparkled with tears as she looked up at him while Janie promised her life to Nathan. He squeezed her hands in his, blessed beyond measure that Liza had chosen him.

She repeated her vows. "I take thee, Rob Darcy, to be my wedded husband, to have and to hold from this day forward, for better for worse, for richer for poorer, in sickness and in health, to love, cherish, and to obey, till death us do part."

The swell of emotion wouldn't be contained, and he had to clear his throat.

Her return smile was tremulous. And then the preacher pronounced them husband and wife.

Rob cupped Liza's jaw and brushed a kiss across her lips. Applause rose from their guests as they turned to face the crowd.

He leaned close to whisper, "Nathan has a surprise."

JANIE FOUND her joy *could* grow beyond what she'd known only this morning.

Nathan had hired a photographer all the way from Denver, Colorado, to take several tintypes of the wedding party.

When she protested the expense, he only laughed and kissed her.

"I want to remember this day for always," he said.

Looking up at his joy-filled expression, so did she.

The only gray cloud was Mindy's absence. Though Nathan had written and invited her, her answer had been an unequivocal *no*. Janie prayed daily for the relationship to be repaired, but only time would tell if Mindy softened toward her half-brother.

Nathan didn't let go of Janie, even when the photographer tried to separate them, even when the family laughed.

And then when everyone else had walked down the boardwalk to the shop to partake of the wedding cake Mama had made, Nathan pulled her to a stop.

She looked at him questioningly, and he pulled a small paper-wrapped package from behind his back. "The tintypes weren't the only wedding gift."

"What? Nathan..."

His boyish grin melted her heart. "Here."

She unwrapped the paper to discover a small music box.

"Nathan." She studied the beautiful piece, imagined what it must have cost. "You shouldn't have. It's too much."

He bussed a kiss on her cheek. "You're my wife. Spoiling you is my prerogative."

His wife.

After what she'd been through in Cottonwood Cove, she'd never thought to hear the words.

She'd never expected Nathan. Hadn't known a love so pure and true existed.

She tilted her chin up, inviting a kiss, which he eagerly supplied. She stayed in his arms, content beyond anything she'd ever felt.

When he pulled away, reminding her in a whisper that they were expected, she couldn't help hugging him close once more.

"I love you," she whispered.

"I love you, Janie. For always."

"For always."

ALSO BY LACY WILLIAMS

WIND RIVER HEARTS SERIES

Marrying Miss Marshal

Counterfeit Cowboy

Cowboy Pride

The Homesteader's Sweetheart

Courted by a Cowboy

Roping the Wrangler

Return of the Cowboy Doctor

The Wrangler's Inconvenient Wife

A Cowboy for Christmas

Her Convenient Cowboy

Her Cowboy Deputy

Catching the Cowgirl

The Cowboy's Honor

SUTTER'S HOLLOW SERIES (CONTEMPORARY ROMANCE)

His Small-Town Girl

Secondhand Cowboy

The Cowgirl Next Door

LOOKING BACK, TEXAS SERIES (CONTEMPORARY ROMANCE)

10 Dates

Next Door Santa

Always a Bridesmaid

Love Lessons

THE SAWYER CREEK SERIES (CONTEMPORARY ROMANCE)

Soldier Under the Mistletoe

The Nanny's Christmas Wish

The Rancher's Unexpected Gift

Someone Old

Someone New

Someone Borrowed

Someone Blue (newsletter subscribers only)

The Bull Rider

The Brother

The Prodigal

COWBOY FAIRYTALES SERIES (CONTEMPORARY ROMANCE)

Once Upon a Cowboy

Cowboy Charming

The Toad Prince

The Beastly Princess

The Lost Princess

Kissing Kelsey

Courting Carrie

Stealing Sarah

Keeping Kayla

Melting Megan

HEART OF OKLAHOMA SERIES (CONTEMPORARY ROMANCE)

Kissed by a Cowboy

Love Letters from Cowboy

Mistletoe Cowboy

Cowgirl for Keeps

Jingle Bell Cowgirl

Heart of a Cowgirl

3 Days with a Cowboy

Prodigal Cowgirl

NOT IN A SERIES

Wagon Train Sweetheart (historical romance)

Made in the USA
Middletown, DE
13 July 2021

44115723R00149